Stranger With a Gun

Cal Dawson, privileged son of ranch owner Clem Dawson, was fast gaining the reputation of a hellion. He was a man twisted by trouble, and always left wanting more. Trouble was exactly what he got when he led a murderous bank raid in the town of Bitter River. Confident he had gotten away with the crime, he did not reckon on the diligence of Sheriff Steve Manders.

Now Dawson finds himself awaiting trial in Manders's custody – to the fury of his influential father who arranges a jailbreak. But then Cal makes his second mistake by abducting Manders's girl.

The feud can be resolved only in violence and death and the scene is set for a bitter showdown between the Dawsons and the young sheriff.

Stranger With a Gun

William S. Corby

A Black Horse Western

ROBERT HALE · LONDON

© John Glasby 2005
First published in Great Britain 2005

ISBN 0 7090 7753 X

Robert Hale Limited
Clerkenwell House
Clerkenwell Green
London EC1R 0HT

Typeset by
Derek Doyle & Associates, Shaw Heath.
Printed and bound in Great Britain by
Antony Rowe Limited, Wiltshire

CHAPTER ONE

BANK RAID

It wanted less than an hour to dawn when the four riders reined up their mounts on the riverbank. At this time of the year the river was almost dry, a stony bed with scarcely a foot of water flowing over it. The river marked the northernmost boundary of the Double K spread. On the other side, facing the men, four miles away was the town of Bitter River. At their backs, beyond the ranch, lay a narrow range of pine-covered hills and then the alkali flats of the Badlands.

One of the men kicked his mount forward a few paces ahead of the others. He sat tall and easily in the saddle, clean-shaven, his hat on the back of his head. The guns at his hip rested in well-worn holsters.

Over the years, Cal Dawson, son of the man who owned the big Double K spread, had gained a reputation as a hellion, a man twisted by trouble and wanting more.

The three men at his back were of the same breed.

All of them were gunslingers hired by his father.

Cal sat staring out into the darkness where Bitter River still slept in almost total darkness. Then he turned abruptly.

'You're certain that shipment came in on the stage yesterday, Hal?'

Hal Jensen, the Double K foreman, gigged his horse forward until he sat alongside the other. 'It arrived all right. I was there like you said. I saw them take it into the bank.'

Cal's features suddenly took on an expression of almost fanatical satisfaction.

'Then I reckon it's ours for the takin', boys. And all of you remember what I said. We just take the money, not the gold.'

At the rear, Matt Calder slipped cartridges from his belt and inserted them smoothly into the chambers of his Colts.

'Why do we have to leave all that gold, Cal? Hell, that could set us all up for life.'

'Damn you, Calder.' Cal snapped. 'Ain't I made myself clear? It ain't no part o' my plan to go on the run with every Federal marshal on my tail for the rest o' my life. We can spend those dollar bills without any questions bein' asked. But gold bars are different.'

Normally, he might not have considered this daring robbery. But over the past six months he'd lost a whole heap of money gambling in the saloon. Now it was time for pay-back. Unless he wanted these debts to be brought to the attention of his father. And he had no doubt as to what the outcome of that would be. A blazing argument and he'd probably be disowned.

Whatever happened, he wanted control of the spread when the old man died.

The men he'd played poker with were professional gamblers and he knew better than to mess with them. They had powerful friends in Tucson who could make life difficult for him if he reneged on the deal. Once it got around that his IOUs were worthless he could find himself in real trouble.

'You figger there'll be any interference from the sheriff and his deputies?' Torran, a hard-featured man, asked.

Cal deliberated on that for a few moments, then shook his head. 'They won't be expectin' anything. Anybody intent on getting their hands on that shipment would've gone for the stage. Nobody will reckon on us takin' it in broad daylight.'

'If the sheriff does show up, I'll be ready to take care of him.' Jensen growled. His voice was a deep mutter low in his throat. 'I've had too many run-ins with Manders. It'll be a pleasure to send his soul to hell.'

Cal swung on him, his face hard. 'I don't want any more shootin' than necessary.' His tone held a hint of iron. 'We go in fast and get out fast. You got that?'

He knew he could trust these men implicitly. Not only to carry out any orders he gave but also to keep any of this from his father. It was essential that the other should never suspect he was in on anything like this.

Not that his father had always been averse to stepping outside of the law. There had been something in the old man's past about which he never spoke; something to do with an episode during the recent Civil War.

Whatever it had been, he always did his best to stay

7

on the right side of Sheriff Manders.

A chill wind blew up with the faint brightening of the false dawn. It gusted around them, striking from all directions, rustling eerily in the stunted thorn-bushes. Lighting a cigarette, Cal drew the smoke deep into his lungs. He'd spent several days making sure his plan for getting his hands on the money in the bank were fool-proof.

At exactly 8.50, Clive Donalds, the bank manager, arrived at the front door to open up for the day. The two cashiers came five minutes later on the dot. After that, business went on as usual. But this time it was going to be different.

They would ride into town quite openly. All of them were well known. Then, with their faces covered, Cal felt certain no one would recognize them. Once they got away, they'd head into the hills. There was an old mining-camp there which only he knew about.

He didn't doubt that most of the townfolk would believe it was some outlaw gang that had staged the robbery. Even if some might suspect their identity, there would be no way they could prove it.

'Soon be sun-up.' Calder remarked, breaking the uneasy silence.

Cal checked the watch which reposed in his vest pocket.

'Another hour before the bank opens.' He tossed his cigarette butt away. 'We don't want to hang around town too long. That could be dangerous.'

Clive Donalds made his way slowly along the boardwalk as he did every morning during the week, regular as clockwork. It was almost a quarter to nine but already the town was awake with people opening up the stores which lined both sides of the solitary street.

The stage had arrived the previous day with the monthly shipment of money for the bank. It was always a day of worry for him. Even though few people knew when it was carrying this kind of cargo, the information somehow got around and there was always the possibility of the stage being held up somewhere along the trail from Tucson.

On this occasion the amount of money and gold on board had been larger than usual and he'd spent an apprehensive half-hour waiting outside the bank while it had all been taken inside and stored in the safe. But everything had gone off without a hitch.

A quick glance along the street told him that everything appeared normal. A bunch of riders had reined up just outside the hardware store twenty yards away but he gave them only a cursory glance as he paused outside the door of the bank. He took the key from his pocket, inserted it into the lock, opened the door and went inside.

The outer office of the bank was only small with the railed counter along the side furthest from the door. Business was usually slow nowadays, not like it had been some twenty years earlier when he had first come to Bitter River. Then there had been gold mined in the hills bordering the town.

It had brought quite a number of prospectors to the area. But the mining-camp had closed down almost twelve years before and the workings had been left to rust. Now only the ranchers and storekeepers used the bank on a regular basis.

With these thoughts running through his mind, he pushed open the half-door at the side of the counter, stepped through, then paused abruptly as the street door opened. He expected to see his two assistants entering. Instead, four men came in, their faces masked with bandannas. Two had guns in their hands.

Instinctively, Donalds' hand reached for the gun just inside the counter.

'Don't try it, old man.' Cal rasped. 'Unless you want to get your head blown off.'

The faint sunlight slanting through the windows glinted off the Colt in his right fist. He held it with the barrel lined on the bank manager's head.

Donalds snatched back his hand as the other came forward quickly. He was no fool. This man meant every word he said. He retreated a couple of steps as Cal reached in and took the gun. Jensen and Torran moved towards him, leaving Calder standing just inside the doorway, out of sight of anyone in the street.

Leaning forward, Cal said in a voice like the lash of a whip: 'Now move back there and open that safe. Do just as you're told and nobody gets hurt.'

'You'll never get away with this.' Donalds blustered. 'The sheriff is only a few yards away and—'

Cal prodded the gun barrel hard into the manager's back.

'Reckon you'd better pray he doesn't butt in.'

The menace behind Cal's words was not lost on the other. He moved his right hand slowly, taking no chances with the gun in his back, and fished the large key from his pocket.

Not once removing his gaze from him, Cal called:

'Anythin' suspicious out there in the street?'

Calder half-turned and shook his head.

'There are a couple of men comin' this way,' he hissed harshly. 'Looks like they may have business here.'

'Those are my two cashiers.' Donalds said quickly. 'They always come in at this time.'

Cal pushed the gun harder between the other's shoulders.

'Not a sound,' he ordered, 'or the three of you are dead.'

Motioning to Jensen and Torran, he waved them towards either side of the door. A couple of seconds later, the cashiers came in. They froze instantly as Jensen and Torran lined up their weapons on them.

'Don't try anythin' foolish,' Jensen warned. 'Move over there to the wall.'

Lifting their hands, the two men did as they were told. One look at their faces told Cal they would have no trouble from them. He turned his attention back to Donalds.

'Now get that safe open and be quick about it if you want to stay alive,' he snapped.

The safe was one of the old-fashioned kind, not one of the newer combination safes. He watched intently as the manager inserted the key, twisted it, and pulled the thick steel door open.

'Bring those bags.' Cal ordered.

Jensen moved around to the back of the counter. While Cal held his gun on the manager, he reached inside, grabbing the bundles of bills and stuffing them into the three canvas bags they had brought with them.

For a moment, Jensen eyed the gold bars stacked neatly against the back of the safe. Inwardly, he still felt Cal was being foolish not to take them while they had the chance.

'Just the money,' Dal said, as if divining his thoughts. 'That gold ain't of any use to us.'

Reluctantly, Jensen straightened. 'That's all of it,' he muttered.

'Good.' Cal nodded. 'Now let's get outa here before any o' the townsfolk decide to come.'

Against the wall, Donalds said tautly:

'There ain't nowehere you coyotes can run. The law will catch up with you sooner or later. Then you'll find yourselves danglin' from the end of a rope and—' His flow of words was stopped abruptly as the butt of Cal's Colt crashed against the side of his head.

He slumped limply against the wall, his legs twisted beneath him, his eyes closed.

'What do we do with these two?' Jensen asked, gesturing towards the cashiers.

'There ain't no way we're goin' to talk,' one of them stuttered.

'Too damned right you're not.' Jensen stepped forward, levelling his gun on the man.

For a moment, Cal considered letting the foreman shoot them. There was a lot at stake here. Then he spoke sharply.

'No need to kill 'em.' To Calder, he called: 'Toss me that rope you brought.'

He caught it in one hand and forced the two cashiers to kneel on the floor, their backs together. Swiftly, he bound the rope tightly around them, finishing by gagging them both,

'Looks pretty quiet outside,' Calder called from the doorway.

'Then let's go before all hell breaks loose,' Cal replied.

One after the other they ran through the door and across the dusty street towards the waiting horses. From somewhere behind them came a woman's shrill scream. A bullet hummed through the air close to Cal's head as he reached his mount. The horse shied violently as the slug ricocheted off the wall of the nearby building. Fighting the animal savagely, Cal pulled himself into the saddle.

The other three men were already on their mounts, pushing them to a gallop towards the end of the street. Cursing, Cal tightened his grip on the reins and kicked spurs into the animal's flanks. More shouts erupted and from the corner of his eye he spotted the sheriff emerging from his office, the two deputies on his heels.

Several shots followed him as he bent low in the saddle to present a more difficult target. Another twenty yards and he would be on the trail leading into the hills.

Someone suddenly appeared on the boardwalk ten yards in front of him. He had a fragmentary glimpse of a white-whiskered face and a shotgun gripped in the oldster's hands. The gun roared as the man pulled the trigger.

Instinctively, Cal flung himself sideways and down as the shot blasted over his head. Almost without him knowing it, the bandanna across his face slipped and fell down on to his neck. With a supreme effort, he tightened his grip on the reins with his left hand, pulling himself upright.

His right hand jerked the Colt from its holster as he swung swiftly and loosed off a couple of shots at the man, knowing with a sickening certainty that the other had seen and recognized him in the instant his face had been visible.

He wheeled his mount on to the hard-packed dirt of the trail and risked a quick look behind him. The old man had ducked into a doorway: his shots had clearly missed.

Cursing under his breath at his bad luck, Cal urged his mount along the track at a breakneck speed. His companions were now several yards ahead.

Cal had been prepared for a posse being hurriedly collected and knew those men would be on their trail within minutes. But once inside the pines which grew in profusion on the lower slopes of the hills, he had figured they could throw any pursuers off their trail.

This had all been part of his plan. So far, everything had gone just as he'd hoped, except for that last piece of bad luck when the old-timer had recognized him.

While Jeb Forrest and Slim Benson, the two deputies, hastily went to get a posse together, Steve Manders, the sheriff, ran quickly along the boardwalk, then across the street to the bank building. Thrusting his way inside, followed by a knot of the townfolk, he found the two cashiers tied and gagged against the wall.

Behind the counter, he came upon Donalds' unconscious form.

'One o' you men get Doc Marsden and bring him here,' he shouted to the bystanders. Swiftly, he untied the two men and helped them to their feet.

'What happened?' he asked tautly.

'There were four of 'em,' muttered one of the men haltingly. 'They were all inside the bank when we got here. They slugged Mr Donalds and then tied us both up.'

A groan from Donalds brought Steve whirling round. He bent beside the other.

'What was taken?' he said.

Donalds put a hand up to his head. For a moment, his stare was unfocused. Then he twisted his lips into a tight grimace of pain as he tried to collect his thoughts.

At last he said thickly:

'They just bust in as I opened up, Sheriff. Held me up at gunpoint and forced me to open the safe.'

'They get away with much?'

Donalds nodded weakly. He tried to get up but Steve pushed him him back.

'Just stay where you are until the doc gets here. You've had a pretty hard knock. Now, how much was taken?'

Donalds licked his dry lips.

'That's the funny thing, Sheriff. They took all of the money but the leader said they weren't interested in the gold. Reckon they left that.'

Steve furrowed his brow. That didn't make any sense. Any outlaw gang intent on robbing the bank would take everything they could lay their hands on. Clearly, this was a well-organized raid. Those men knew that the stage had brought in the shipment the previous day and had planned this for exactly the right time.

Instead of holding up the stage somewhere along the trail, they had waited until its cargo had been safely deposited in the bank.

It was just possible this robbery had been staged by someone in the nearby territory rather than by outlaws from across the border. Clearly, that was something he'd have to look into.

Just as he approached the door someone rushed in. He recognized the man immediately: Seb Butler. Butler was well into his eighties, one of the original gold-prospectors who had remained in Bitter River after the others had drifted on.

'Glad I got you, Sheriff,' Butler said in a wheezing tone. 'Them critters that just held up the bank . . .'

'Yeah, what about 'em?' Steve asked.

'I took a shot at one of 'em just before he hit the edge of town.'

'Did you hit him?'

'Nope.' Butler shook his head emphatically. 'But I got a glimpse of his face when his bandanna slipped off as he ducked in the saddle.'

'You recognized him?' Whatever the oldster said, Steve knew he couldn't place too much credence on his testimony. Butler was a character around the town, spending most of his time begging for drinks off the customers in the saloon in return for wild tales of the old days.

'I'm pretty sartain, Sheriff. I reckon it were Cal Dawson.'

A look of surprise spread over Steve's face.

'I reckon you'd better be damned sure of that, Seb.

Clem Dawson is a mighty powerful man in these parts. I'd need a lot more proof than that before I went accusin' his son of bank robbery.'

As he moved past the old-timer, Steve heard the other mutter:

'Ain't nothin' wrong with my eyesight. I know what I saw.'

Outside his office, Steve found that the posse had been gathered. Eight men, together with Slim Benson, were in the saddle waiting for him.

'Where'd you reckon they'll be headed, Sheriff?' asked one of the men.

'Up yonder into the hills,' Steve replied. 'I doubt if they'll try to cross the alkali flats. Too dangerous. But they may try to hole up for a while, or cut west towards the Tuscon trail.'

'All right,' Benson said. 'Let's ride.'

The trail leading into the hills was narrow, winding and tortuous. Most of the way they had to ride in single file and for the first mile, it was possible to follow the marks of the robbers in the dust.

Further on, however, they encountered bare rock and here they lost the trail. Raising his hand, Steve called a halt.

'Reckon there ain't much point goin' on much further,' he said harshly. He pointed towards the towering crests of the hills. 'There are too many tracks and old Indian trails yonder and they could've taken any of 'em.'

'Could be if we head west we might cut 'em off before they reach the Badlands,' suggested one of the riders.

'Not much chance of that,' Steve was forced to admit. 'They've got too much of a start on us. We'll head back to town. I want a word with Cal Dawson when next he rides in.'

Having reached the abandoned mining-camp, Cal slid from the saddle, then moved to the edge of the wide ravine. It would be easy to pick out the sound of approaching horses from a mile or so in the distance.

At last he was satisfied that if a posse had been sent out from town they had lost their trail far down the track. He went back to the others and gestured them inside.

'Reckon we're safe here,' he said tersely. 'There ain't nobody in town knows where this place is except for that old fool, Seb Butler and I'm goin' to take care of him. He must have seen my face after he'd taken a shot at me.'

'You reckon he knows who we are and could talk?'

'Could be. Fortunately, most folk reckon he's been touched in the head ever since this seam ran out twenty years ago. Even if the sheriff does listen to him, I doubt if he'll believe him.'

Jensen and Torran laid the heavy bags down in the middle of the room.

'What do we do now?' the foreman asked.

Cal grinned broadly. 'Quite simple. We divide this five ways. I get two and you get one each.'

'Why not divide it four ways?' Jensen argued. 'We're all in this together.'

Cal gave him a menacing glance. 'Whose plan was it?' he demanded. 'If you'd gone into this by yourselves, do you reckon any of you would've had the brains to pull it off so well?'

Still grumbling, they divided the bills as Cal had dictated, laying them out on the table.

'All right,' Cal grated. 'Now we stash most of this here. Ain't nobody likely to come nosyin' around this place and we can't afford to be found with all this money on us.'

Torran lifted his brows into a tight line.

'And what's to stop one of us ridin' up here and makin' off with the rest?'

Cal's lips twisted into a tight grin.

'I reckon if that happened he's likely get a bullet in his back.' He ran a quick glance around the room, then nodded towards the large iron stove against the wall. 'That's as good a place as any.'

Once the money had been placed inside the stove they rode back to the Double K, taking a circuitous route down the western slopes of the hills, well away from the town.

As they rode into the courtyard Clem Dawson stepped down from the long veranda and came towards them, his face grim.

'Where the hell have you been, Cal?' he demanded curtly. 'You been gone all night.'

Cal stepped down from the saddle.

'Like I told you last night, we had to ride out to the south edge to check on that fencing,' he said easily. 'We've already lost several steers.'

There was a bright speculative glint in the older man's eyes. 'Reckon you'd better tell that to the sheriff,' he said. 'He's inside right now askin' some questions.

Seems the bank in town was held up this mornin'.'

Cal climbed the steps and nodded nonchalantly.

'Can't see what that has to do with us, Pa. We ain't been within ten miles o' town.' He glanced round at his three companions. 'Ain't that right, boys?'

'Sure thing,' Jensen said. The three of them nodded in agreement.

Inside the house, Cal found the sheriff in the front room. He was standing next to the window. It was evident he had watched them ride in and had gauged the direction from which they had approached the house.

'Somethin' on your mind, Sheriff?' he asked, keeping his voice even and casual.

Steve turned. 'Just checkin' up on a few things,' he said shortly. 'I understand you've been out all night. Mind tellin' me where you were?'

Cal lowered himself into a chair and crossed his legs. 'As it happens, me and three of the boys were out at the south end of the spread. Some of the fencin' needed repairing.'

'In the dark?'

Cal thought fast. He knew the sheriff was no fool and there was something in the other's manner which told him that Seb Butler had already spilled what he had seen.

'We started late yesterday afternoon, worked until nightfall. Since there was still some work to finish we decided to make camp there and finish it at first light.'

'I guess that explains things, Sheriff,' Clem Dawson said from the doorway. 'I reckon you have to ask questions but I sure don't like the idea of you comin' here and suggestin' my son had anything to do with this robbery.'

Steve threw a quick glance from Clem to his son. He felt a little rise of anger at the smug expression on Cal's boyish features.

'Problem is,' he said thinly, choosing his words with deliberate care, 'we got a witness who claims it was Cal leadin' that bunch.'

He saw Clem stiffen perceptibly. The rancher's face hardened into taut lines. Through thinned lips, Dawson demanded:

'Just who is this witness, Sheriff?'

'Seb Butler. Reckons he fired at the leader just before he hit the edge o' town. Unfortunately, he missed or we might have that *hombre* in the morgue by now.'

'Seb Butler!' Dawson spat the words out. 'Why that old coot couldn't recognize anyone on the other side o' the street. He's just a crazy old loon who'll spin any yarn so long as he gets somebody's attention. You ain't makin' him out to be a credible witness, are you?'

'Reckon not,' Steve said as he walked towards the door. 'But if I were you, I'd keep Cal out of town for a while. If Butler tells his story often enough, some o' the townsfolk might get around to believin' it.'

CHAPTER TWO

BITTER RIVER

The town of Bitter River was beginning to come alive after the oppressive heat of the day. The air was still warm and there was little coolness in the wind that blew off the Badlands to the south, stirring little eddies of dust along the street.

Making his way along the boardwalk, Steve kept a watchful eye on the place. A bunch of riders from the Double K had ridden in half an hour earlier, all of them the usual riders for the ranch. Evidently they intended to make a night of it in one of the town's two saloons.

The Horseshoe saloon just twenty yards ahead of him was full of noise. A woman's voice hammered out one of the songs from the Deep South to the accompaniment of a tinny piano.

Steve paused, then pushed open the batwing door and went inside. He hadn't seen Cal Dawson ride in with the others but he was keeping an eye open for trouble. At the moment, he didn't know what to make of Seb Butler's story. Even if he arrested Cal on a charge of robbery, he doubted if any jury would believe the old-timer's rambling tale. All he could hope for at the moment was that Cal or one of the others might let something slip.

He recollected that there had been some trouble a while back when Clem Dawson had bought the Double K spread five miles out of town. Rumour had it that he'd purchased it with money made from selling stolen arms to the South during the Civil War. Several men had been killed when that gang had attacked wagon trains carrying weapons along the trails between North and South. And since most of the townsfolk were Northerners from back East, there'd been a heap of ill-feeling at the time.

Things seemed to have settled down, however. Now the only trouble came from Cal Dawson. A hellion with a temper like a rattler, who relied on his father's influence to get him out of trouble.

Hitching his gunbelt a little higher about his waist, Steve crossed to the bar. The singer finished her song and disappeared off the small stage to a round of applause.

Leaning his shoulders against the counter, he turned and allowed his gaze to roam over the customers.

There was a card-table in one corner with five men seated around it, playing poker. With a sudden stab of apprehension, he noticed one of them was Cal Dawson. Evidently he had ridden in some time during the late afternoon. He sat with his cards held close to his chest.

Two men, both of whom he recognized from his visit

to the ranch that morning, stood immediately behind him.

'What's your pleasure, Sheriff?' The bartender had sidled along the bar and now stood at his back.

'Whiskey,' Steve said quietly.

When it came, he took the bottle and poured some into the glass. 'You expectin' trouble, Sheriff?' the bartender asked.

'Could be. How long has Cal Dawson been in?'

The other glanced across at the card-table, then looked quickly away as he saw Cal's gaze on him.

'More'n a couple of hours, I guess,' he said in a low voice. 'Came in alone. Those other two men joined him a little while ago.'

Steve shrugged. Evidently Clem Dawson wasn't going to heed his warning about letting his son loose in town. Steve pressed his lips into a tight line. If any of the townsfolk got to thinking there might be some truth in what old Seb Butler claimed, it might not be long before trouble erupted.

He was suddenly aware that several of the men ranged along the bar were eyeing him closely. How many of them were friends of Cal's, he didn't know. Inwardly, he figured they'd stay out of it if the other started any trouble. But those two hired hands were there for a purpose.

He sipped his drink slowly and forced himself to relax. The pianist finished his solo, gave a flourish on the keys, and the singer came back on to the stage again.

Motioning to the bartender, Steve bent forward.

'Are there any more of Dawson's men in tonight?' he asked softly.

The other shook his head. 'Ain't seen any. Couple left a while ago. Mebbe they're at the Lonesome Trail saloon. You reckon—?' He broke off sharply.

The saloon doors had opened and Seb Butler came in. A warning tingle started along Steve's spine as if there were a gun pointed at him from the shadows. He tried to ignore it but the feeling grew as Butler walked slowly towards the bar.

It seemed that the old man hadn't noticed Cal sitting at the table in the shadowed corner for he didn't glance in that direction. But one look told Steve that not only Cal, but the two men standing behind him, had spotted the octogenarian. Their eyes followed him intently as he crossed to the bar.

Butler edged up beside Steve, resting his gnarled hands on the counter. Gesturing to the bartender, Steve told him to give the old man a glass and poured a liberal measure into it.

'Why thanks, Sheriff,' Butler wheezed. 'That's mighty generous of ye.' He took a swallow of the whiskey, wiped the back of his hand across his whiskers. 'Have ye thought any more about what I told ye? I—'

There came an angry shout from the other side of the room. The card-table was suddenly overturned and crashed on to the floor, scattering the playing-cards. Cal Dawson was on his feet. His face twisted in anger, he strode towards the bar, his face flushed, thrusting a couple of men out of his way. It was apparent he had already drunk more than was good for him.

He thrust his face close up to Butler's grizzled features. 'I hear you've been makin' certain allegations about me, Butler,' he rasped. His tone was low and

25

deadly. 'Mebbe you'd care to repeat 'em to my face.'

For a moment, Steve thought the old-timer was about to back down. Then Butler spoke hoarsely.

'I know what I saw, Dawson,' he said. 'Mebbe you reckon I don't see too well these days. But it were you all right. Guess I only—'

'Why, you lyin' skunk.' Cal's right hand dropped towards his Colt. 'I ought to shut your big mouth for good. Nobody gets away with callin' me a bank-robber.'

His gun was almost clear of its holster when Steve stepped forward.

'Back off, Dawson,' he said. 'I thought I'd given you fair warnin' this morning but it seems you're hellbent for trouble.'

Cal glanced at him and there was an ugly glint in his narrowed eyes.

'It ain't me come lookin' for trouble,' he muttered thickly. 'But if this sidewinder don't keep his mouth shut, I'll make sure it's shut permanently.'

'You ain't scarin' me none, you young whippersnapper,' Butler said. 'I've seen men like you afore, seen 'em come and go.'

Cal's face twisted into a mask of wild fury.

'This time you've gone too far, old man,' he snarled. His left hand lashed out and gripped the other by the throat, fingers gouging deeply into the scrawny flesh.

'Stand away from him,' Steve said, pushing himself away from the bar.

'You stay outa this, Sheriff.' Cal spoke thickly through his teeth, not once taking his glance from the old man. 'I don't take bein' branded a lawbreaker from any man.'

'I said stand away from him, or I'll be takin' you in to cool off in the jailhouse.'

'You don't scare me none, Sheriff. You're just foolin' yourself if you reckon you're the law around Bitter River.' His grip on Butler's throat tightened even further. The old prospector's eyes bulged in their sockets and a gasping wheeze escaped from his constricted throat.

Without hesitating, knowing that in his present state of mind, Cal meant to kill the old man, Steve drew his gun, reversed it, and brought the heavy butt down on Cal's wrist.

Dawson staggered back, grasping his arm with his good hand. His lips thinned back over his teeth like an animal's.

'You've busted my wrist,' he roared.

'Just be thankful I didn't put some lead into you,' Steve told him coldly. Out of the corner of his eye, he saw the two hired hands moving forward, their hands dropping towards their guns.

Almost quicker than the eye could follow, Steve's Colt was lined up on them.

'Make one wrong move and you're both dead men,' he said tautly. 'Now you two get on your mounts and hightail it back to the Double K before I change my mind.'

'What about Cal?' growled one of the men.

'He stays here. I'll have Doc Marsden look at that wrist of his. Mebbe Butler ain't got things right but I'm holdin' him on suspicion of being the leader of that gang that robbed the bank this mornin'.'

'You got no proof o' that, Manders,' Cal hissed

savagely. 'That old fool is touched in the head. He'll say anythin' so long as there are others just as foolish as you to listen to him.'

'We'll leave it to a jury to decide that,' Steve snapped. 'It's only a week before the circuit judge gets here. Reckon you won't come to any harm until then. There are quite a few people who reckon you're guilty.'

Still covering the two men, Steve stepped forward and unfastened the gunbelt around Cal's waist. He placed it on the counter. He jerked his head towards the two men.

'Now you two do like I said. Get on your mounts and ride back to the ranch. Tell your boss I've got his son locked up in jail. You can also tell him there ain't no way Cal is goin' to get out of this one until we have a trial. Got that?'

Both men nodded sullenly.

Once the sound of their departure had died away, Steve turned his attention to Cal.

'Now move,' he said flatly.

'You'll never keep me in jail,' Cal rasped as he staggered away from the bar. 'Once my father hears about this, he'll wreck this whole town.' He grinned viciously. 'And you'll be the one danglin' from the end of a rope.'

'We'll see about that,' Steve replied. Prodding the gun barrel into the other's back, he walked him to the door and outside into the street. 'See to it that Butler is all right,' he called over his shoulder. 'Give him a couple of drinks.'

Inside the saloon, everything had fallen quiet. Even the pianist seemed unable to continue with his act.

Steve thrust open the door of his office and forced

Cal inside. Jeb Forrest had just stepped through the door at the back leading to the cells. Slim Benson was seated in Steve's chair, his legs crossed on top of the desk.

'What the hell. . . ?' Slim began, jerking himself to his feet.

'I'm lockin' up this polecat on suspicion of being involved in that robbery.'

Forrest reached for the cell keys and led the way along the short passage. He pushed open one of the cell doors. Steve thrust Dawson inside, slammed the door shut and locked it.

'This is goin' to cause a whole heap o' trouble once Clem Clawson hears of it,' Forrest muttered.

'Too damned right it is,' Cal shouted from inside the cell. 'He'll see to it that all three of you are strung up.'

Steve ignored him and returned to his office. 'Get Doc Marsden here to take a look at that wrist of his,' he said to Forrest. 'I don't reckon he'll be usin' that hand for some time.'

Once the deputy had gone, Steve put up his feet on the desk and stared morosely at the ceiling. He didn't underestimate the trouble he could expect from the boss of the Double K. Several times in the past Cal had caused trouble in town, usually brawling in the saloon after he had drunk too much.

But this was something far more serious. Clem Dawson would never stand for his son standing trial on a charge of suspected bank robbery. Very soon, all hell would break loose in town unless he could do something to prevent it.

Benson hung the cell key on the wall, then swung to

face him. 'You reckon that was a wise thing to do, Sheriff?' he said echoing Steve's thoughts. 'Bringing Cal in. Even if you do hold him until the circuit judge gets here, Clem will hire some fancy lawyer and he could easily get a dozen men to swear he was at the other side of the spread, nowhere near town when that robbery took place.'

'Mebbe so. But from what I saw tonight, Cal would've killed Butler if I hadn't stopped him. He tried to strangle the old man. To my way o' thinking, there's a lot more truth in what Butler said than some folk believe.'

Benson shrugged and lowered himself into a chair.

'I just hope you know what you're doin'. Clem Dawson is a bad man to cross and he has some mighty powerful and influential friends in town.'

The street door opened at that moment and Forrest came back with the doctor. There was a third figure immediately behind them. Mary Marsden came in and closed the door behind her.

'Are you all right, Steve?' she asked anxiously, coming over to the desk and looking down at him. Her clear-cut features showed a deep concern in the yellow lamplight.

'Sure, I'm fine, Mary,' he replied. 'Just a little trouble with Cal Dawson.'

'Where is he?' her father asked.

'Take the doctor through, Slim,' Steve said. 'And keep your hand near your gun. He might try to make a break for it.'

Mary waited until the deputy and her father had gone to the cells before turning to face Steve.

'Don't you think that was a stupid thing to do, Steve?

30

Now you've made an enemy of Clem Dawson. You and I are to be married in a couple of months – if you live that long.' There was a note of accusation in her voice. It quavered a little and there was the shine of tears in her eyes.

'I've sworn to do my duty as sheriff, Mary. You know that. I can't let a man get away with robbery even if he is Clem Dawson's son.'

'And if it wasn't him? You're going to look a fool.'

'Makes no difference. Call it a hunch if you like, but right now, I'm danged sure he was the leader of that gang,' Steve said tautly. 'And so long as I'm sheriff, no one robs the bank and gets away with it.' There was a note of finality in his tone which Mary recognized at once.

'But you can't be certain he was with that gang. All you've got is the word of one man and he certainly isn't what I'd call a reliable witness.'

'Then why did he try to throttle the only man who could testify against him?'

'Maybe it was just anger at Seb for saying it. You know the kind of temper Cal has. This isn't the first time he's tried to kill someone with his bare hands.'

The doctor came back five minutes later.

'I've fixed him up as best I can, Steve,' he said, placing his bag on the desk. 'Reckon he'll live until the judge gets here.'

At the Double K ranch, Clem Dawson was seated on the veranda smoking a cigar when the two ranch hands rode into the courtyard and slid their mounts to a halt. One glance at their faces in the light that spilled through the open door told him something was wrong. Whenever they and Cal went out for a night in town it was usually a little before dawn when they arrived back. He heaved himself to his feet and walked down the steps.

'Somethin' wrong?' he called loudly. 'Where's Cal?'

'Locked up in the town jail, boss,' one of the men answered.

Dawson felt a momentary surprise but it was gone in an instant. He was well aware of his son's reputation. Twice within the past year he'd had to bail him out for brawling in one of the saloons.

'What the hell is it this time?' he asked, tossing the cigar butt away.

Neither man seemed inclined to answer and he was forced to repeat his question.

'Sheriff Manders arrested him for that bank robbery this mornin'.'

'Robbery?'

'That's right, boss. Cal tried to silence Seb Butler when he accused him of it. He's keepin' him there until the circuit judge gets here.'

The other man spoke up. 'I reckon he'll—'

'Shut up, the both o' you,' Dawson roared. 'I've got to think this out.'

He walked back to the veranda and stood staring into the darkness. Somewhere at the back of his mind was a nagging little suspicion. It might just be the kind of thing Cal would do, expecially if he was in desperate need of money. With an effort, he pushed the idea out of his mind.

'Shouldn't be too difficult to bust Cal outa jail,' Matt

Calder said. 'Manders has only two deputies to back him up. If we was to ride into town with a bunch of the boys, I guess we could make that sheriff change his mind.'

'That may be so,' Dawson muttered. 'But if word got to the federal authorities, we're in trouble.'

The last thing he wanted was some federal marshal riding into town and asking a lot of awkward questions. If they poked around enough and discovered a tie-in between himself and the illegal trade in guns with the Southern forces during the war, it could spell prison for him.

'So what do you aim to do?'

'I'll take care of the sheriff in my own way,' Dawson said at last. 'You two saddle up again and come with me. The sooner I have a talk with Manders, the better.'

They rode into town half an hour later and reined up in front of the lawman's office.

Dawson swung himself from the saddle and strode up the steps. He thrust the door open and went inside. The two men followed him, taking up their positions on either side of the door.

Steve glanced up quickly as they came in. He gave a slight nod.

'I've been expectin' you, Dawson,' he said quietly. His gaze took in the rancher's bulky frame and also the hired hands.

'Too damned right you have, Manders.' The rancher walked forward until he was standing over the desk. 'And you know why I'm here.'

'If you've come to try to get your son out o' jail, I'm sorry I can't accommodate you.' Steve kept his tone low and even. 'There's a witness who claims your son was the leader o' that bunch.'

'Now see here, Sheriff,' Dawson said, 'I came here to try to be reasonable. I can make your job here as sheriff an easy one or a hard one.'

'Meanin' that if I was to turn a blind eye to what's happened, you'd make it well worth my while?'

Dawson shrugged. 'From what I know, bein' a lawman don't pay too good. You lay your life on the line for the citizens of this town every day and where does it get you? They'll get rid of you when they figger you're too old and put someone else in your place.'

Steve's smile was strained and tight as he faced the rancher over the desk.

'I figured you'd do a lot o' things, Dawson. But I didn't reckon you'd try to bribe a sheriff.'

'Every man has his price.' Dawson't lips stretched into a smile but there was no mirth in it. 'There are plenty of lawmen who're doin' fine just so long as they know who their friends are. I understand you're marryin' Mary Marsden in a couple of months time. We wouldn't want anythin' to happen to spoil that.'

Steve felt his fingers clench tightly on the edge of the desk.

'If you've got any ideas of harmin' Mary, or her father, forget 'em. Believe me, Dawson, it'd be the last thing you do. This territory wouldn't be big enough for you to hide.'

Dawson placed his large hands on the desk top and leaned forward. He stared at Steve, his eyes glinting dangerously. 'I'm just sayin' that accidents do happen.' His voice dropped even lower. 'You're gettin' yourself into big trouble, Sheriff. As for makin' this robbery charge against Cal stick, just remember this. There ain't a single man in this town who'll testify that it was him. And I've got men back at the ranch who'll swear he was nowhere near Bitter River when it happened.'

Steve's lips thinned into a hard, straight line.

'Ain't you forgettin' he sure as hell would've killed Seb Butler if I hadn't stopped him? I was there. I saw everythin' that happened.'

'So you say,' Dawson snarled. 'I don't reckon your word will count a lot against a dozen honest citizens of this town. You ain't exactly been on good terms with Cal in the past. Some folk might think this is your way of gettin' back at him.'

'Think what you like,' Steve retorted. He was having difficulty in controlling his anger. He guessed the rancher was deliberately trying to provoke him into going for his gun. Out of the corner of his eye he saw the two men near the door lower their hands slowly towards their guns. Dawson straightened.

'I want to see Cal,' he grated. 'Get his side o' the story.'

Steve got to his feet. 'All right.' He jerked his thumb towards the two men at the door. 'They stay here where my deputies can keep an eye on 'em and you leave your gun on the desk.'

For a moment, the rancher seemed on the point of arguing. Then he nodded to the ranch hands and laid his gun on the desk top. 'Keep a close watch on those two, Jeb,' Steve said.

Forrest gave a nod, levelling his rifle at the men.

Cal Dawson was lying on the hard iron bunk in the

cell. He swung his legs to the floor as the two men approached.

'You've got a visitor,' Steve said harshly. Turning to Clem Dawson, he added: 'Make it quick.'

'You come to teach this lawman a lesson and get me out, Pa?' Cal said insolently. 'Do you think I was part of that gang that raided the bank?'

'No, I don't,' Clem said. 'But don't you worry none. I'll see to it there's no evidence against you once the circuit judge gets here. Just tell everythin' as it happened to Cy Rawlins. You'll be outa here in a couple o' days.'

'I wouldn't bank on that,' Steve snapped. 'Mebbe your pa reckons he can bribe or frighten Seb Butler against testifyin' to the truth, but somehow I doubt it.'

The rancher swung on him savagely, teeth bared.

'I don't have to do anythin' like that, Manders. Once Rawlins does the talkin', ain't no judge in this territory is goin' to convict him.' He turned back to Cal. 'Just trust me, son,' he went on. 'I'll have you out o' here by tomorrow.'

Clem Dawson stalked out of the office with the two men close behind him. From the window, Steve watched as the three men approached their mounts. He guessed they intended riding back to the ranch but instead, Dawson said something to his companions and, unhitching their horses, they walked them along the street in the opposite direction.

Forrest came up beside him. 'Where d'you figger they're headed, Sheriff?' he asked.

'Not to the saloon,' Steve said. 'My guess is they're

goin' to have a talk with Cy Rawlins.'

A host of thoughts and half-formed ideas were chasing themselves around in his mind.

The lawyer had been implicated in a number of crooked deals in the past and Steve suspected he'd had a hand in getting that ranch for Dawson.

He had no doubt the man was as crooked as they came but there was no denying he was both clever and cunning, with a talent for twisting the truth to his own and his clients' advantage.

Forrest made himself a smoke. He struck a sulphur match on the doorpost, lit his quirly and blew the smoke out in front of him.

'You want me to follow him and see where he goes?'

Steve considered that, then shook his head.

'Dawson's no fool. He'll be expectin' me to have him watched. He's got some plan in mind but right now, I can't figger out what it is. You'd better turn in for the night. I'll keep an eye on our prisoner.'

Dawson tethered his mount to the rail and walked up to the door of Rawlins's office. The place was in darkness but that did not put him off. He knew that the lawyer had his rooms above the office.

Glancing along the street in both directions to make sure there was no one in sight, he hammered loudly on the door. Less than a minute later a light showed in one of the upper windows.

'Who the hell is that?' Rawlins's voice called down to them. 'Don't you know what time it is?'

'It's Clem Dawson. Just get down here and open this door.'

There was a short pause, then the lawyer replied:

'All right. Just give me a couple o' minutes.'

Dawson waited impatiently. The run in with the sheriff had brought no better edge to his temper. Now, as he stood waiting, the lines around his mouth deepened.

There came the sound of a key being turned in the lock and the door swung open. It was evident that the lawyer had been asleep and he did not take kindly to being wakened at that hour of the night. Seeing Dawson standing there with the two men at his back made him choke back on his irritation. Dawson pushed his way inside.

'I want to talk to you, Rawlins,' he said sharply.

'Won't it wait until the morning?'

'No. This is important. It can't wait.'

Shrugging, Rawlins led the way into the front room and placed the lamp he had brought with him on the table.

'Very well, what is it you want?' He turned the lamp up a little.

'I reckon you've heard about the bank hold-up this mornin'.' Dawson seated himself in one of the chairs at the table.

'Of course.' The lawyer nodded his head. 'Just what has that got to do with me? Sheriff Manders is the law in this town. I merely prosecute anyone suspected of breakin' the law.'

'Yeah. Only this time he's got my son in jail on a charge o' holdin' up the bank.'

Rawlins's brow furrowed at that remark.

'Cal! They reckon he was in on it?'

'That's right. That crazy old fool Seb Butler claims he

shot at one o' the gang. Says it were Cal.'

The lawyer sat for a minute staring down at his hands. His thin lips pursed into a serious line. Eventually he looked up.

'And he's sure it was Cal?'

'Not only that. He's spreadin' it around town,' Dawson said. 'But you don't have to worry none about him. I've got my own plans for makin' sure he won't be around to testify at any trial. The problem is that Manders believes him. He claims Cal tried to kill Butler in the saloon tonight.'

'That could be a problem,' Rawlins agreed.

Dawson nodded. 'That's why I'm here. I'm relyin' on you to get him out before the circuit judge gets here.'

The lawyer pondered that for a few moments. Then he scraped back his chair, went over to the cupboard, and came back with a bottle of whiskey and two glasses. He set them down on the table, filled the glasses and pushed one towards the rancher.

'What you're askin' ain't going to be easy, Mr Dawson. Besides, even if I did get him out on a point o' law, he'd still be a wanted man. If he tried to hightail it outa town, Manders would soon round up a posse and be close on his heels.'

'I'll take care of that.' Dawson downed his drink in a couple of swallows. He leaned forward over the table. 'Manders ain't no fool. It doesn't matter how much you twist the law, he ain't goin' to let Cal go.'

'Then how. . . ?' Rawlins ran his tongue over his lips.

'You're goin' to do exactly as I tell you.'

CHAPTER THREE

BREAKOUT!

It was a little after eight the next morning when Jeb Forrest entered the sheriff's office. Steve was seated behind the desk, drinking coffee.

'You been awake all night?' the deputy asked.

Steve gave a nod. 'Nothin' much happenin'.'

'Reckon you'd better go across to the hotel and get yourself a bite to eat. I'll take over. You might as well get a few hours' sleep too.'

Gratefully, Steve finished his coffee, then got to his feet. 'There shouldn't be any trouble from Clem Dawson. He's got somethin' in mind but I reckon he ain't foolish enough to try to bust Cal outa jail.'

'Yeah. But don't forget Cal's got a few friends in Bitter River. They might try somethin'.'

'He's also got some enemies too.' Steve walked to the door, then paused. 'You might also get a visit from that fancy lawyer wanting to talk to his client.'

'Do I let him talk?'

40

'Sure. If Dawson wants to waste his money on that shyster that's up to him. Just make sure you're there while he's talkin'.'

As he strode across the street and along the far boardwalk, Steve tried to figure out what Dawson intended to do. The rancher had tried to bribe him into letting Cal go and forgetting the whole incident.

When that had failed, he had tried threats, not only against himself, but against Mary and her father. Yet somehow, he doubted if Dawson would bring his boys into town and try to shoot it out.

One or two of the men who worked for the rancher were probably born killers but the majority were just hard-working riders, unlikely to go against the law.

Throwing a quick glance along the street, he pushed open the hotel door and found himself a seat in the dining-room. He deliberately chose a table near the window where he could keep an eye on everything going on outside. Ordering bacon, eggs and strong black coffee, he leaned back in his chair and rolled himself a smoke while he waited.

It had been a long night. Half an hour after he had seen them heading along the street, Clem Dawson and his two hands had ridden out. None of the men had even glanced in the direction of the jail.

Through the window, he had glimpsed the rancher's face as he had ridden past. There had been a smug, satisfied expression on it. Evidently his talk with Rawlins had proved satisfactory. What they had cooked up between them, Steve couldn't guess. But that look had increased his apprehension. There was something in the wind and undoubtedly Cy Rawlins was in on it.

41

The noise from the saloon had soon picked up again after he had left with Cal Dawson. It had continued until well into the small hours.

In the cell along the passage Cal had remained quiet throughout the night. Some of his earlier bluster had gone out of him and he'd probably decided to let his father do whatever was necessary to get him out of jail.

Steve's breakfast came and he ate ravenously. Halfway through it a sudden movement on the opposite boardwalk caught his attention. He recognized the man immediately. Cy Rawlins hurrying along in the direction of the jail.

Evidently Dawson had got through to him and no doubt he'd listened to all the lies and denials Cal told him. One thing was for sure. Rawlins wasn't the type to try any heroics. He would simply be Dawson's mouthpiece at the trial. While pretending to uphold the law, he'd do his best to twist it in an attempt to get Cal freed.

He finished his meal, pushed the empty plate away and built a smoke. The coffee was hot and burned his tongue but it brought a little of the feeling back into his limbs. Yawning, he sat back. Maybe it would be better if he got some sleep. At the moment it was difficult to think clearly.

He got up and threw a further glance through the dust-smeared window just in time to see Mary and her father walking in the same direction as Rawlins. Probably going to check on Cal's smashed wrist, he guessed.

He lit the cigarette, inhaled deeply and went outside, where he leaned his shoulders against the doorpost. The sun had risen, throwing long shadows across the street. At the moment, everything seemed quiet. A couple of the stores were just opening up.

Five minutes later, Rawlins emerged from the office at the far end of the street. Half-way back to his own place, the lawyer glanced up, squinting against the sun. Then he turned abruptly, stepped down into the street, and walked across to Steve.

'Glad you're still up, Sheriff,' he said casually. 'I heard you've had a long night. I'd like a word with you, if I may.'

'That's all right by me,' Steve replied. 'Step inside.' It seemed odd that Rawlins could have anything to say which could be of interest to him. But he decided to hear him out.

'In my office, if you don't mind.'

Shrugging, Steve fell into step beside the other. He noticed at once that the lawyer seemed ill at ease, unsure of himself, and wondered why. Once or twice, the man glanced back over his shoulder, perusing the street.

'You had your talk with Cal Dawson?' Steve asked.

Rawlins nodded. 'That's what I'd like to talk to you about.'

As they reached the lawyer's office, Rawlins took a key from his pocket. He unlocked the door of his office, motioned Steve inside and closed the door behind him.

'Take a seat, Sheriff. This won't take long.'

Placing his hat on the small desk by the window, Rawlins sat down. He gave Steve a hard, bright glance, took a cigar from his pocket and lit it with a sulphur match, inhaling deeply.

'I had a visit from Clem Dawson last night,' Rawlins

said, speaking through the cloud of blue smoke.

'Somehow I figured you would,' Steve remarked drily. 'Once he found out he couldn't bribe me into lettin' that hellion go.'

'I've listened to what Cal has to say,' Rawlins said. He fiddled with a sheaf of papers in front of him. 'He could be lyin', of course. But if all you've got to rely on is what Seb Butler says, and those ranch hands at the Double K back up Cal, it ain't goin' to be easy gettin' him convicted of robbery.'

'And you're goin' to do your best to see that he isn't.'

Rawlins sat back in his chair. 'I reckon I should make my position quite clear, Sheriff. Dawson has paid me well to defend his son. I don't have to believe he's innocent or guilty. I'm not responsible for what any of those witnesses say in court. After they've heard all of the evidence, it'll be up to the jury to decide.'

Steve thinned down his lips. 'Doesn't it strike you as strange that there were four men in that gang and Cal claims he was out with three of his father's hands all night?'

Rawlins shrugged nonchalently. 'Coincidence. That won't stand up in court. It's up to you to do your duty as you see fit, Sheriff. But I'm afraid you won't—' He broke off sharply.

There was a sudden sound outside. It was barely audible but Steve's keen hearing picked it up immediately. It sounded like a single shot but one which was oddly muffled. It was followed almost at once by a babble of yells and then the unmistakable sound of a horse being spurred into the distance.

Almost knocking over his chair, Steve lunged to his

feet and walked swiftly to the door. He threw a swift glance along the dusty street.

A small knot of men were running towards his office. Without pausing, he ran along the boardwalk. The office door was open. Tugging his Colt from its holster, he walked through to the cells. Jeb Forrest lay slumped against the wall, a spreading red stain on the front of his shirt.

A couple of feet away, the doctor lay face down on the floor just outside the cell. The cell door was open and there was no sign of Cal Dawson.

A moment later, someone came running along the passage and stopped just behind Steve. It was Slim Benson.

'What the hell. . . ?' the deputy gasped. 'I thought I heard a shot but I couldn't be sure.'

Steve checked on Forrest, feeling for the pulse but the deputy was dead. Then he turned his attention to the doctor. There was a nasty wound on the back of his head but he was still breathing.

'Help me get him into the office,' Steve said harshly, his voice like an iron bar. 'I don't reckon he's hurt bad and he's the only one who can tell us what happened.'

Benson bent and together they carried the doctor's unconscious body from the passage, laying him gently in one of the chairs. Once this was done, Steve examined the scalp wound. Clearly, the doctor had been hit with a gun butt but whatever had been used, he doubted if it was a Colt.

'Get me a rag and some water,' he said without looking up.

Once these came, he cleaned most of the blood away.

As he had surmised, the wound was too small to have been made by a heavy gun. Scarcely had he finished than Marsden uttered a low groan and opened his eyes.

For a few moments there was an unfocused stare in them. Then he struggled to push himself upright.

'Mary,' he gasped. 'Is she. . . ?'

'Just sit where you are, Doc,' Benson said firmly. 'We don't want to start that wound bleedin' again.'

'I'm all right, but you've got to get after Cal. He must have taken Mary with him.'

Steve jerked back at the words. A sharp rush of anger and apprehension raced through his mind. For a moment, he stared across the doctor at Benson.

'Get some men together, Slim,' he ordered tautly. 'And make it quick.'

The deputy hurried out of the office and Steve turned back to the doctor.

'What the hell happened in there?' he demanded. 'How did Cal get out?'

'The critter had a gun – a derringer. Don't ask me how he got it. He pulled it on us just as Forrest opened the cell door to let me in. He shot the deputy when he tried to draw on him. He said he'll kill Mary if you go after him.'

Steve nodded. 'Go on.'

'Then he told Mary to walk out in front of him. That was just before he slugged me.'

Helping the doctor to his feet, Steve kept a tight grip on his arm as the man swayed. His mind was whirling. It was all beginning to fall into place now and he cursed himself for being such a fool as not to have seen it coming. Only one person could have slipped that derringer to Cal – Cy Rawlins!

No wonder the man had seemed edgy and ill at ease. It had all been a well thought-out and executed plan that Dawson and Rawlins had cooked up between them the night before. And just in base he butted in at the wrong moment, Rawlins had deliberately taken him to his office to keep him there until everytihng had gone according to plan.

Five minutes later, Slim returned. Six men sat their mounts outside near the rail. After checking that Marsden was all right, Steve went out, buckling his gunbelt a notch tighter. His own mount stood ready at the hitching rail.

'Guess some of you know what's happened,' he called loudly. 'Cal Dawson broke outa jail and he's taken Mary Marsden with him. Any of you who reckon he wasn't in on that bank robbery can forget it. Now he's wanted for killin' one o' my deputies.'

'Where do you reckon he's headed, Sheriff,' asked one of the men. Steve swung up into the saddle.

'Somehow, I don't think he'll head back to the Double K. He knows that would be the first place we'd look.'

'Could be he'll hightail it to the Mexico border,' suggested another man.

Steve shook his head. 'He's no fool. He knows he'd never get there, especially not with the girl. Every lawman in the territory would be on the look-out for him.' He reached a sudden decision. 'We ride for the Dawson spread. He must've stashed that money he stole somewhere. He won't leave without it.'

Leaving Bitter River, the posse rode south, taking the

wide trail that skirted the hills. They rode quickly, keeping an eye out for both Cal and any of Clem's men who might be watching the trail.

Less than half an hour later they came within sight of the ranch house. There were several men in the courtyard but no sign of Cal. Steve rode up to the doorway.

'Dawson!' He called the rancher's name loudly.

Almost a full minute passed before Dawson appeared in the doorway. He held a Winchester in his hands.

'What do you want here, Manders?' He stepped down from the veranda. 'You're trespassing on my land.'

Steve smiled thinly. Somehow, he managed to keep the blazing anger inside him in check.

'Your son broke outa jail this mornin', shot and killed one of my deputies. That sure makes him a wanted killer now.'

A flicker of expression gusted over the rancher's hard features. It was only momentary, gone in an instant.

'I know nothin' of any jailbreak,' he rasped. 'And if you're lookin' for Cal, you won't find him here.'

'Then you got no objection to a couple o' my men takin' a look around?'

Dawson hesitated for a second, then shrugged.

'They can look all they want to. They won't find anythin'.'

Steve signalled to two of the riders who dismounted and went into the house. Then he swung his gaze back to Dawson.

'Reckon you don't seem too surprised to hear o' this breakout, Dawson.'

'What do you mean by that?' The rancher glared at him and lifted his rifle a little higher.

'Just that it was Cy Rawlins who slipped a derringer to Cal. Weren't nobody else near the jail so it had to be him. And the two of you were in mighty close cahoots last night.'

For a moment, Steve thought Dawson meant to bring the Winchester up and train it on him. Then the rancher thought better of it and took a tight grip on himself.

'Mebbe you got proof it was Rawlins. Cal has a lot o' friends in town. Any of 'em could've done it.'

Steve grinned viciously. 'Reckon it won't be too hard to get that crooked lawyer to talk. Once he does, it'll tie you in with conspiracy to murder and kidnapping.'

This time there was a clear look of surprise on Dawson's features.

'I don't know what you're talkin' about. Who's been kidnapped?'

'As if you didn't know.' It was one of the posse who spoke. 'Mary Marsden, the doctor's daughter. She was taken when your son broke jail. Now he's got her holed up someplace. Mebbe he figures on using her as a hostage to save his own neck.'

'You're lyin',' Dawson grated. 'Cal might be a high-spirited hellion, but he doesn't fight with women.'

The two posse men came out of the house shaking their heads. They moved towards the barn as Steve pointed. Somehow, he felt certain neither Cal nor the girl were here. Clem wouldn't dare risk having a federal marshal brought in. There might be too many awkward question for him to answer.

It seemed more than likely Clem didn't know her whereabouts. Even if he did, they'd never get it out of him.

The two men came back ten minutes later. It was clear they had found nothing. Steve waited until they climbed back into the saddle, then lowered his gaze until it rested on the rancher.

'This ain't finished, Dawson.' There was barely controlled anger in his tone. 'Your son can't run for ever. I'll get him and when I do, he'll be tried and hanged for this day's work.'

'Wherever he is, you'll never find him,' Dawson sneered. 'Even if he is on the run, he knows this territory better than anyone.' Turning to go back into the house, he called over his shoulder: 'I did give you a fair chance, Manders. If you'd listened to me, none o' this would've happened.'

Steve wheeled his mount with a savage jerk on the reins. Leading the posse back along the trail he waited until they were out of sight of the ranch house before holding up his right hand and calling a halt.

He swung in the saddle and said harshly:

'It's obvious Cal ain't at the ranch and I doubt if he'll head for the border. That's well over a hundred miles to the south. Any of you men know of any other place wnere he could hide out?'

'Ain't likely he'll head into the Flats yonder,' grunted the nearest man. 'That'd be sheer suicide. A man wouldn't last more'n a couple of days out there.'

Steve nodded. 'That only leaves the hills.'

'Hell.' Benson stared at him. 'You ain't thinkin' of scouring those hills for him, are you? There must be

50

more'n a score of old trails leadin' through them, most of 'em leadin' nowhere. He could've taken any one of them.'

'Surely there must be some place he could hole up in until all of this has died down,' Steve protested.

There was a short silence, then another of the men spoke.

'There's an old mining-camp there. But it's been deserted for nigh on twenty years.'

Steve experienced a faint surge of hope.

'You know where it is?' he demanded. The man ran a hand over his whiskered chin.

'I've nothin' more than a vague idea. Only been there once and that was over thirty year ago.'

'You reckon you could lead us to it?'

'I guess I could try,' the man replied with a trace of doubt in his voice.

'Good. Then lead the way. There are still a few hours of daylight left.'

At that moment, Clem Dawson sat behind his desk facing the three men who had been with his son during the night before the bank hold-up. The big man with a hard face was Hal Jensen, the Double K foreman, a man whose bulk belied his speed with a gun. A man who had worked alongside Dawson during the war, he was the only man the rancher really trusted.

The other two hired hands were Matt Calder and Herb Torran, both gunslingers with a string of murders to their names stretching back to the Mexico border.

Dawson's hold on all three was as tight as a hangman's noose. He knew that any order he gave would be carried out without question. At the moment, he wanted information.

'Has Cal ever spoken to any of you of some place where he's likely to head for at a time like this?'

Jensen and Calder both shook their heads, remaining silent.

Dawson's penetrating gaze flickered in Torran's direction.

'You know somethin', Herb?'

'Could be,' the other replied. 'Cal and me used to ride into the hills on occasions. We found this old mining-place up there in the topmost ridges. Cal figured there might still be gold there for the takin', though we never found any.'

'And you could find that place again?'

'Sure. I'm certain I could find it. There ain't many folk in town who know of it.'

'Could be you're right about Cal headin' there.' The rancher nodded. 'Makes sense to me. Round up some of the boys and get up there.'

'And if he is there?'

'Bring him back here. Ain't likely Manders will come lookin' in the same place twice.'

The three men headed for the door. Turning, Calder asked:

'And the girl? What do we do with her? She could make trouble.'

Dawson pondered that for a moment. Much as he wanted to see his son safe, his mind balked at the idea of killing women.

'Leave her there. Maybe she'll find her way back into town. If not . . .' He shrugged as if to say her blood wouldn't be on his hands.

Fifteen minutes later, the bunch of riders rode out of the Double K with Herb Torran in the lead.

The tall hills lifted all about them as Steve and the posse rode into them. Massive firs covered much of the lower slopes and the trail they had taken was narrow and tortuous, twisting in and out of the wooded areas in a series of acutely angled bends so that they were forced to ride in single file.

A couple of creeks crossed their path but, although swift-running, the water was not deep and they negotiated them without much difficulty. Up ahead, louring cloud hid most of the upper levels from view.

Most of the way they rode in an uneasy silence. Steve sat tensely in the saddle, allowing his mount to pick its own way. Was their guide right when he had spoken of this abandoned camp high up near the crests? If he was wrong, they were wasting precious time chasing a fantasy.

'It won't be easy gettin' up there,' said Benson suddenly from just behind Steve.

'Somebody must've used this trail in the past,' observed another man.

'Probably an old Indian track they used to cross the hills,' Steve replied. 'As for those who worked this old mine, they most likely used burros. If Cal did come here, he must be pretty sure of himself.'

Leaning forward to enable his mount to gain a better footing on the treacherous ground, Steve gripped the reins tightly as the horse forced its way through tangled thorn that partially blocked the way. Some raked across his face as he fought his way on.

The only thought in his mind was to locate this camp. At the rate they were progressing, the sun would be close to setting by the time they got there. A little while later, the trail angled sharply to their right and they emerged on to a stretch of more level ground.

In places, however, it was broken and eroded and it took them the best part of half an hour before they were all safely at the end.

'How much further?' he asked irritably. The man in front reined his mount and turned.

'Far as I can recall, it should be about a mile further on.'

Steve made to answer him, then held up his hand sharply for silence.

'What is it, Sheriff?' Benson spoke in a low voice. 'You hear somethin'?'

'Thought I picked up the sound of horses.' Steve turned his head slowly. This time there was nothing and he began to think he'd been mistaken, or had it been merely his imagination?

Then the sound came again and this time he managed to gauge its direction. It came from somewhere to their left and below them. There was now no doubt. Quite a sizeable group of riders, he estimated, and they were spurring their mounts fast, regardless of the treacherous trails.

He motioned to the others to remain where they were, dismounted, handed the reins to Benson and slipped into the thick underbrush at the edge of the track. This could mean trouble, he decided tensely, but exactly where and from whom, he wasn't sure.

Easing the Colts in their holsters, he pushed his way through a mass of brush, picking his way carefully, for here the ground sloped steeply away from the track.

He passed through a stand of tall trees, and came out on to the lip of a precipitous drop where the ground shelved steeply downward for forty feet. He lowered himself on to his stomach and wormed his way to the edge. At first, he could see nothing. Then, where the slowly setting sun glinted through gaps in the clouds, he made out the patch of dust and, a second later, spotted the riders. They were strung out in a long file, urging every last ounce of speed from the horses, regardless of the danger.

To his way of thinking, there could be only one explanation. Somehow, Dawson had also figured out where Cal might be. It wasn't beyond the bounds of possibility that at least one of his men also knew of these mine-workings and the rancher had put two and two together and come up with the most logical answer.

Gritting his teeth, he followed the others as they swung around a bend in the other trail. For a few moments, they were out of sight. When they reappeared, he clearly made out the big man who rode in the lead. Recognition was immediate. There could be no mistaking Hal Jensen, the Double K foreman, even at that distance.

He turned swiftly. Taking care not to be seen, he worked his way back up the slope to the others.

'Trouble?' muttered Benson. Steve gave a nod.

'Big trouble. Somehow Clem must've got wind of this mining-camp and he's sent a bunch of his men up there.'

'Damn. How close are they?'

'Close enough. They're pushing their mounts to the limit. Ain't no doubt they'll get there afore we do.'

The deputy drew his lips together into a hard, straight line.

'What now?' he asked tautly.

'We go on,' Steve told him. 'We've got no choice. I reckon we can be sure where Cal and Mary are. At least we'll have the element of surprise.'

He swung into the saddle and set his mount running forward at a gallop.

Some thirty minutes later, the trail led into a wide canyon. There was a shallow stream running diagonally through it and on the far side, a large wooden shack stood against a sheer wall of rock. The canyon walls enclosed it on three sides and the location of the old building meant that it could not be attacked from the rear.

CHAPTER FOUR

RESCUE AT GUNPOINT

There were eight horses standing in front of the building but no sign of their riders.

From what Steve could see, it appeared that the mine had been a fairly prosperous place and at one time there must have been a goodly number of miners working the seams. Evidently little of it had been done by panning. These men had dug for gold. Over to one side a couple of shafts stood boarded up. Now, however, the planks covering them were warped and splintered.

The posse dismounted and moved their horses back for some distance down the trail where they were out of sight. Crouching down behind a large rock, Steve surveyed the scene intently. Over on the far side, a couple of narrow trails cut back through the rock and it was evidently along one of these that the other riders had come.

One of those mounts would be Cal's, he decided. That meant Clem Dawson had sent seven men out to look for him. Obviously, he was taking no chances.

'If we try to take 'em from the front, we'd never have a chance,' Benson, beside him, murmured softly. 'It would be a massacre. They'd cut us down from inside before we covered ten yards.'

Steve cast a worried glance at the sky.

'It'll be dark soon and that won't make it any easier. Our only chance will be to spread out among the rocks and wait until they come out.'

'Could take a while,' Benson replied. 'Depends on what orders Clem Dawson gave those men.'

Steve signalled to the rest of the posse and watched as they worked their way along the canyon wall, keeping their heads down. It was possible that none of the men inside were aware of their presence. But at the forefront of his mind was the nagging question of what they intended to do with Mary.

If they decided to take her with them, she would still be able to testify against Cal. The thought that they might decide to silence her permanently made him grit his teeth in anguish. A feeling of utter helplessness swept over him. Angrily, he forced it away. Thinking along those lines could be fatal.

At the moment, all they could do was sit it out and wait for the men inside the shack to make their move.

Slowly, the minutes passed and still there was no sign of any activity from the shack. Outside, the horses were getting restive.

'Reckon we'll have to make our move soon, Sheriff,' Benson grunted.

Steve nodded in reluctant agreement.

'Cover me. I'm goin' to try for the shack,' he said, getting his legs under him.

'Don't be a fool, Sheriff. If they have anyone watching at the windows, they'll shoot you down before you get half-way there.'

'Then I reckon that's a chance I'll have to take.'

He sucked in a deep breath, thrust himself around the rock and sprinted along the canyon wall, expecting at any moment to hear a gunshot. But, incredibly, none came. Clearly, the men inside hadn't considered the possibility that the location of this place was known to anyone else. For all they knew, he and the posse had ridden straight back to town from the ranch.

A minute later, he threw himself down hard against the far wall of the canyon some ten yards from the side of the cabin. Gasping air into his lungs, he slowly heaved himself upright. There was only one small window facing in his direction. The glass had long since fallen out, leaving nothing but a square hole in the wall.

He edged cautiously towards it and pressed himself against the wooden wall. A moment later, he caught the sound of voices from inside.

One he recognized as Jensen's. It sounded harsh and urgent.

'You've got to see sense, Cal. You can't stay holed-up here for ever without food and water. And if we was to bring it to you, it wouldn't be long afore someone got suspicious and decided to follow us. Your pa's orders are that you ride back with us.'

'And have that sheriff on my neck with a noose

waitin' for me?' It was Cal Dawson who spoke this time.

'The sheriff's already been out to the ranch and searched it from top to bottom. There ain't much of a chance he'll return. By now, he probably figgers you're half-way to the border. Ain't no reason you can't hide out on the spread until we can figger some way of gettin' you across into Mexico.'

A pause, then: 'And what about the girl? We can't let her go. She knows too damned much.'

'Why the hell did you have to bring her along? That was a damnfool thing to do.'

Steve froze as he heard Cal snigger.

'I figured it might be fun. Steal the sheriff's gal before he can marry her. Besides, if Manders did get lucky and find me, he'd think twice if I had her as a hostage.'

'Well, you sure landed yourself in a whole heap o' trouble,' Jensen retorted. 'Now, are you goin' to do as your pa says or make a bigger fool of yourself?'

The ensuing silence lasted for a full two minutes. Then Cal spoke.

'So what do you propose we should do with her?'

'Your pa says to leave her here. That way we ain't responsible for what happens to her. Somehow, I can't see her ever makin' her way to town on foot.' A pause, then: 'You've got enough blood on your hands, Cal.'

'All right. We do as he says.' There was a reluctant note in Cal's voice. 'But you'd better be right about the sheriff not comin' back to the ranch, otherwise there'll be a gunfight. I ain't goin' to let anybody take me alive. Let's saddle up and get outa here.'

Steve picked up the sound of heavy footsteps inside

the cabin. Swiftly, he pulled the Colts from their holsters and tensed himself with his shoulder hard against the wood. Slowly, he moved forward a couple of feet.

A moment later, he heard the door open with a squeal of protesting rusted hinges.

The next second, gunfire broke out from the men along the canyon rim. Steve heard the savage impact of slugs hitting the front wall. Risking a quick look around the edge of the building, he saw two of the men suddenly stagger, arch back on their heels, and go down.

The rest of the men turned and made a mad rush for the door with the exception of two who broke away and set off at a run towards the horses. They threw themselves down and returned the fire.

Steve pulled his head back as more gunfire erupted from the shack as the remainder began firing from the comparative safety of the front windows. Gritting his teeth, Steve pondered his next move.

From inside, Jensen's booming voice was shouting above the rest.

'How the hell did they know you were holed-up here?'

'That goddamned sheriff ain't such a fool as we thought,' Cal called back. 'Just let me get him in my sights and I'll put an end to it. Leave this to me. I'll get us all outa here.'

A second later, he shouted: 'Do you hear me, Manders? Better tell your men to put up their guns or the girl gets it. We're comin' out now and there'll be a gun to her head. The first wrong move you make and I'll kill her.'

Steve felt a shiver pass through him at the other's words. He didn't doubt the man meant every word he said. With one killing on his slate, a second would make no difference.

'You hear me, Manders?'

For a moment there was silence. Then Benson's voice yelled.

'We hear you, Dawson.' The gunfire along the canyon ceased abruptly.

'That's better. We're comin' out now. We're all goin' to ride outa here and we'll be takin' Mary Marsden with us. If you want her to stay alive, you won't get any foolish ideas about followin' us.'

For a moment, Steve hesitated. Then, making no sound, he reached up and pulled himself through the window. He dropped lightly to the floor and padded across the small room towards the half-open door on the far side.

Through a crack in the door, he saw Cal bending in the middle of the room. Mary lay on the floor, her wrists and legs bound by lengths of rope. Cal had a knife in his hand with which he sliced through the ropes, then hauled the girl roughly to her feet.

He thrust the knife into his belt and drew a gun which he had evidently taken from one of the other men. He placed it against the side of Mary's head.

In the dimness, Steve caught a glimpse of her features as Cal hustled her towards the door. He kicked it open with his foot, stood on one side and motioned the men outside.

'I'm comin' out now, Manders. If you want the girl to be around for the wedding, you'd better keep all o' your men in check.'

Thrusting Mary in front of him, he stepped through the door, a broad grin on his face. A couple of feet from the door, he suddenly stopped.

'Where are you, Manders? I want to get a good look at you. I know you want to kill me so let's see if you're as good with a gun as I am.'

'I'm right here behind you, Dawson,' Steve said in a quiet, deadly voice.

At the unexpected sound of his voice, Cal whirled, swinging round his gun in the same movement. His hard features were set into a mask of stunned surprise. Before he could bring his gun to bear and squeeze the trigger, the Colt in Steve's right hand spouted muzzle flame, the slug taking the other in the chest.

For a second Cal stood there, swaying. His eyes held a deadly glint of feral hatred as he struggled to hold life in his body long enough to get off a shot. Somehow, he managed to squeeze the trigger. The slug took a sliver of wood from the door near Steve's head. Then Cal's knees buckled and he fell sideways, eyes staring sightlessly in his head.

Without pausing to think, Steve leapt forward, grabbed Mary around the waist and pulled her inside the shack. Most of the Double K men were running for their mounts as the men along the canyon opened fire again.

One of the running men halted in mid-stride. The gun in his hand dropped from nerveless fingers as he toppled sideways. His limp body landed on the boards above one of the shafts. The top collapsed as the rotten wood splintered beneath him and an instant later, he dropped out of sight into the depths. The rest hesitated.

Pressing Mary against the door, Steve stepped out into the open, his Colts covering the men.

'Drop your guns,' he ordered sharply. 'You don't have a chance. This place is completely surrounded.'

Realizing the futility of any further resistance, the Double K riders dropped their guns and lifted their hands. Only Jensen kept his weapon. For a moment, he seemed on the point of using it.

'I said drop it, Jensen,' Steve said, his tone as hard as iron. 'I reckon I could jail three of you for havin' a part in that bank hold-up and the rest o' you for aidin' a man wanted by the law. If you figger on usin' that gun, go ahead.'

'Try it, Jensen.' Benson's voice came from the rocks. 'There are six guns lined up on you. You don't have a chance.'

With a snarl, the Double K foreman let his gun drop.

As the posse came out from the rocks, Steve turned to the ranch hands.

'Cal's dead,' he said. 'Put him across one o' those horses and take him back to the ranch. Now git.'

He waited as two of the men draped Cal's body across the back of one of the horses. Jenson climbed into the saddle.

'You're finished now, Manders,' he called harshly. 'Clem ain't goin' to let this go unavenged. You can't hide behind that badge now.'

Steve held Mary tightly with one arm.

'You tell Clem that once that crooked lawyer talks – and he will, I promise you, he'll find himself in jail,' he called. Steve turned to the men beside him. 'Let them go,' he said. 'That polecat got just what he deserved.'

There had been no compunction in his mind against killing Cal Dawson. Regardless of whether he had held up the bank the man had put himself outside the law when he had shot down Jeb Forrest.

'Are you all right, Mary?' he asked as the last of the Double K riders disappeared along the trail.

She nodded. 'I knew you'd find me somehow,' she answered. There was a little tremor in her voice. 'But how is. . . ?'

'Your father's fine,' he told her reassuringly. 'He just got a knock on the head when that critter escaped. Cal meant to keep you here in case we found him.'

Benson stepped forward, his face grim.

'If that *hombre* Jensen and a couple of the others did ride with Cal to rob the bank, why didn't you hold 'em?'

'Because there's all that stolen money to think about. I'm damned sure they did it. Cal's dead now, so he won't be doin' any talkin'. But if they have that money stashed away someplace, pretty soon they'll lead me to it as long as I give 'em enough rope.'

Benson nodded in understanding. 'Reckon we'd better get back to town, Sheriff. There's goin' to be the devil to pay once Clem Dawson finds out what's happened. He sure as hell won't rest until you're dead.'

'We'll face that when it happens' Steve retorted grimly.

They remounted and put their horses to the steep downgrade.

The main street of Bitter River looked strangely deserted

as Steve and the posse rode in. Darkness had fallen over an hour earlier and the descent through the hills had been slow and arduous.

Doc Marsden was waiting for them on the boardwalk outside the sheriff's office.

As Mary ran to her father, Steve turned to Benson.

'I'm goin' to have another talk with Rawlins. Mebbe he'll open up a little after what's happened.'

'What makes you think that?'

'That lawyer's no fool. He knows this show ain't over yet and Dawson will make damned sure he doesn't talk to anyone about their little conversation the other night. From Dawson's way o' thinkin', Rawlins is an accessory to Jeb's murder.'

'Then surely Rawlins will be more scared of Dawson than anyone,' Benson argued. 'He ain't likely to talk.'

'Mebbe not. But there ain't nothing to lose. The sooner I know what Dawson intends to do, the better.'

Steve tethered his mount and strode off along the boardwalk. Even though there was nobody outside, the saloon seemed crowded as usual. As he reached the batwing doors, he cast a quick glance inside.

The little man in the bowler hat was seated at the piano but at the moment he wasn't playing. Another poker-game was in progress at the table against the far wall. Several men lined the bar, their backs to him. Then, just as he made to move away, he spotted the lawyer in his black coat seated with another man at a small table in one corner.

Steve pushed open the doors and went in, his eyes wary. Some of these men had been Cal's friends and, at the moment, he didn't want any more trouble.

He went over to the table and stood staring down at the lawyer. The stranger sitting with him looked up sharply.

'This is a private conversation, mister,' he began, then noticed the star on Steve's shirt. Swallowing thickly, he pushed back his chair, got to his feet, and moved across to the bar.

'I don't have anythin' to say to you, Manders,' Rawlins said thinly. 'I heard what happened up there in the hills.'

'Guess news travels pretty quickly in these parts,' Steve remarked drily.

'Hal Jensen rode into town less than ten minutes ago. Reckon most folk know how you shot Cal in the back.'

Steve stiffened. He might have guessed Dawson would have put it around like that. He thinned his lips.

'That weren't the way it was,' he said. 'Cal had his gun at Mary Marsden's head and was usin' her as a shield, just like the yeller coward he was.'

Rawlins's thick brows went up a little. His glance slid to one side in the direction of the bar.

Turning his head slightly, Steve followed the direction of the other's look. Jensen was there, lounging against the counter, his back to him, talking with a small group of men.

Steve looked back at Rawlins.

'I'll deal with him later,' he muttered. 'Right now you can answer some questions.' He deliberately kept his voice low so as not to be overheard.

'If you think I'm goin' to tell you anything, you're plumb crazy.'

'Don't try to be heroic, Rawlins. It doesn't suit you.' Steve made his tone sarcastic. 'I'm not here to play games. Dawson knows you're the only man who can connect him with Jeb Forrest's murder and so long as you're alive, you're a threat to him.'

'Dawson knows I won't talk,' Rawlins declared, striving to force confidence into his tone.

Steve gave a grim smile. 'Right now, Jensen's watchin' you. Won't take long for him to put two and two together and suspect you're spilling everythin' to me.'

The lawyer's face turned ashen.

'You're not frightenin' me, Manders,' he blustered. 'Dawson and I know each other too damned well. And there ain't nothin' you can do to me. You're not going to be around long enough.'

'So you reckon Clem's got some plan up his sleeve to get rid o' me?'

'Wouldn't know anythin' about that,' replied the other. 'But you can be sure he's not goin' to rest until you're under the ground at Boot Hill.'

'We'll see about that,' Steve said, getting to his feet. He realized he'd get nothing from the lawyer at the moment. Maybe in a few days, once the lawyer had turned things over in his mind, he would talk.

He went over to the bar and ordered a whiskey. He drank it slowly. He was aware that all eyes in the saloon were on him.

Some distance along the counter, Jensen suddenly spoke in a loud voice.

'Washin' some o' the dust of that trail from your throat, Sheriff? If you've any sense, you'll leave town afore mornin'.'

Steve turned slowly. 'And why is that, Jensen?'

'Because folk in these parts don't take to lawmen who shoot men in the back.'

There was a low murmur from several of the men. Steve noticed it immediately but ignored it. He knew the foreman was trying to goad him into some kind of action. He twisted round, placed his elbows on the bar and surveyed the men in front of him, at the same time watching Jensen from the corner of his eye.

'You men want to know what happened up there in the hills this afternoon? The truth, not the lies Jensen has been feedin' you. Cal Dawson was holed up at the mine-workings where he'd taken Mary Marsden. When we caught up with him, he tried to save his own neck by keepin' a gun pointed at Mary's head.

'Only I happened to be behind him. He turned and tried to put a slug into me but he got one instead.'

'He's lyin',' the foreman shouted. Steve drew back his lips into a tight line.

'Then if you don't believe me, ride out to the Double K and take a look at the body for yourselves.'

A few feet away, Jensen suddenly thrust himself away from the bar. His coarse features were twisted into a snarl.

'You callin' me a liar, Manders?' he gritted. His right hand hovered close to the butt of his Colt.

'That's right.' Steve moved clear of the two men in front of him. 'And if you make a move for that gun, I'll kill you.'

Jensen hesitated. Then he stepped forward, hands bunched into tight fists by his sides.

'You're a big man when you're shootin' men down, Sheriff, hidin' behind the law.'

What came next was almost too swift to be taken in by any of the watching men. Jensen's right arm went back, aiming a blow that would have knocked Steve's head back on his shoulders if it had landed.

With a quick move that took the big foreman completely off balance, Steve side-stepped, ducking his head. Before Jensen could straighten up, Steve caught him with a savage blow just behind the ear.

With a yell, Jenson fell heavily against the bar. He would have gone down but one of the other men caught him, held him upright as Steve waited. Shaking his head, Jensen made to turn away as if all the fight had been knocked out of him. But it was only a ruse to take Steve off guard. The foreman grabbed one of the beer-glasses and hurled the contents into Steve's face.

Half-blinded, the sheriff was momentarily unable to defend himself. A crashing left to his face threw him back, off his feet. He hit the floor hard, struggling to wipe the beer from his smarting eyes. His vision was blurred as he blinked rapidly.

Dimly, he saw the boot that came for his side, felt a lance of pain spear through his body. It felt as if most of his ribs had been crushed. Then Jensen leapt forward on top of him, his hands reaching for his throat.

Sucking in a racking breath, Steve somehow managed to get his right leg beneath him. With a savage heave, he threw the foreman to one side and thrust himself up on one elbow. He was aware that his adversary was already getting to his feet, his face murderous, eyes narrowed to slits and filled with a killing fever.

Jensen was clearly not going to stop until he had killed his man and he intended to do it with his bare hands and his feet. Somehow, Steve managed to push himself up onto his knees.

Grinning savagely, Jensen drew back his foot, hoping to kick Steve in the chest. In the split second before the other's heavy boot came in with all of the foreman's weight behind it, Steve's hands lashed out. Clamping them tightly around the in-swinging ankle, Steve twisted, taking the man with him.

Jensen flew through the air, his arms flailing wildly, and hit the solid wood of the bar. For a moment, he hung there. Then two of the men grabbed him under the arms and lifted him up. Shaking his head, he lunged forward.

Struggling to ignore the agony in his side and chest, Steve succeeded in getting to his feet. His vision slowly came back into sharp focus as he faced Jensen. The foreman's mouth was hanging slackly open. He was gulping air down into his heaving chest but he was still dangerous.

Jenson grabbed a chair, lifted it high over his head, and aimed for Steve's face. But already Steve was moving, side-stepping swiftly. The chair splintered on top of a table.

Before the foreman could turn, Steve's bunched fist smashed into the side of his jaw. The other's eyes rolled up in his head. Knees buckling under him, he fell forward across the table.

Steve swung to face the men at the bar.

'Get him outa here,' he rasped. 'The next time he

wants to make anythin' out of it, he'd better be ready to use his gun.'

He left the bar, and made his way acrosss the street to the hotel. Every bone in his body ached and throbbed. He went into his room, locked the door, poured some water into the basin and splashed it over his face. It stung his skin but it took away some of the dullness in his head. Then he dabbed the side of his scalp where he had hit it against one of the tables when he had gone down.

He took off his gunbelt and laid it on the chair by the bed, then stretched himself out. He doubted if there would be any further trouble through the night but he was taking no chances. Both Colts lay within easy reach of his right hand.

CHAPTER FIVE

HIRED GUNS

Steve stood just outside the hotel, smoking a cigarette. It was an hour after sun-up and the air was taking on some of the heat of the coming day. There was not a breath of wind to stir the dust on the boardwalks.

Some of the ache had gone from his limbs after a few hours of deep sleep but there was still a soreness around his ribs. Briefly, he wondered what Clem Dawson would do now that his son was dead.

Somehow he doubted that the rancher would ride into town with all of his men and force a showdown. Angry as he undoubtedly was, and filled with a desire for vengeance, he would get someone else to do his work for him.

Any other way might attract the attention of a federal marshal. If there was any truth in the rumour that he had been a traitor to the North during the war, it wouldn't take long for that to come out into the open and that would be the end of him.

As far as he knew there were only three gunslingers on the Double K payroll. Hal Jensen, the foreman, Herb Torran and Matt Calder. The rest were just cowboys whose only interest was in herding cattle. Somehow, he didn't think they would want any part in this fight. Jensen was raring for a chance to kill him, particularly after his humiliation of the previous night.

But if they came for him, the townsfolk in general would turn against Dawson. No; if the rancher had some plan in mind it would involve outsiders: men hired to kill and who couldn't be traced back to the man who paid them.

He tossed the butt into the boardwalk and made his way across the street to his office. Slim Benson was seated in his chair when he entered. He stood up quickly.

'Heard about the fight in the saloon last night, Sheriff,' he said gruffly. 'Reckon Jensen had that comin' for some time. Want some coffee?'

Steve shook his head. 'Just finished breakfast,' he replied. 'Now all there is to do is wait for Dawson to ride in.'

'You figger he'll try somethin'?'

'Not openly. Deep inside, he knows what Cal was like. Reckon he's always known he'd end up with a bullet in him or swingin' from a rope. He'll also know that Cal weren't shot in the back like Jensen was tryin' to make out.'

'Mebbe you're goin' to find out right now,' Benson said harshly. He nodded towards the window.

Steve glanced up quickly. Several riders had reined their mounts to a halt just outside. He instantly recognized Clem Dawson at the forefront.

Benson moved swiftly to the wall, picked up a rifle, checked it, then held it ready in both hands.

The door was thrust open and Dawson stormed into the office with a couple of men at his back. There was no sign of Jensen.

'You know what I'm here for, Manders,' Dawson said viciously. 'You killed my son yesterday. I aim to see you pay for that.'

'Your son was a killer,' Steve said, slowly and evenly. 'He shot my deputy when he busted out o' here and he'd have killed Mary Marsden if I hadn't stopped him.'

'I don't give a damn what you say,' Dawson shouted. 'I've heard all I want to hear from my men.' He was clearly holding himself under tight control with an effort. 'Your days as sheriff are numbered. But I'm goin' to make you sweat before you die.'

Steven felt himself tense at the other's words. He knew the man was trying to make him lose his temper and do something foolish.

'And how do you figger on doin' that?' Steve asked thinly. 'Your threats don't scare me none.'

'No?' Dawson stepped forward, placed his hands on top of the desk, and thrust his face close to Steve's. 'I'm givin' you due warnin'. I've already sent word to the Kelton brothers. Reckon you've heard of 'em. They'll be here in Bitter River in three or four days to kill you.'

He uttered a harsh laugh as he drew his head back. 'You won't stand a chance against the five o' them. But just to make certain, the Nangordo Kid will be ridin' with 'em. How does it feel to be a man with a price on his head?'

One of the men standing behind the rancher grinned, showing his teeth.

'Reckon there'll be a nice little shootin' party in town once they arrive, Sheriff. And don't reckon on any o' the townsfolk helping you against them.'

Dawson straightened. He turned to stare directly at Benson.

'I reckon you got a wife and kids. Better think carefully. You want to chance your luck against the Nangordo Kid?'

Benson said nothing.

'No, I guess not.' He turned his burning glance on Steve. 'My guess is you'll be standin' alone when they ride in, Sheriff. And you won't know when they'll come. Like I said, you'll just have to sweat it out until they cut you down.' He turned and strode towards the door, then paused as he reached it. 'And don't even think of makin' a run for it. There ain't any place big enough for you to hide in. I'll have every trail out of Bitter River watched.'

A couple of minutes later, the riders left, leaving a cloud of dust hanging in the air.

Against the wall, Benson lowered the rifle. There was a sheen of sweat on his face.

'You reckon he means what he says?' he asked. 'About the Kelton brothers?'

'He means it all right. Those five outlaws will hire out their guns to anybody who pays enough.'

'And the Nangordo Kid. What about him? They reckon he's wanted all over the territory south of here.'

76

Steve pursed his lips. 'From all I've heard, he's a loner.'

'And also reckoned to be the fastest gun in the territory.' The voice came from the doorway and, glancing up, Steve saw Doc Marsden standing there. 'You don't have a chance goin' up against him.'

'So what am I supposed to do? Hand in my badge and run like a coyote with my tail between my legs?'

'At least that way you'd stay alive.' Mary had come in with her father. 'I heard most of what Dawson said.'

'I have to stay,' he replied simply. It was quietly said but there was the promise of death in the words.

'Then there's nothing I can say or do to make you change your mind? You don't owe this town anything, Steve. Do you think these killers will stop at shooting you once they ride into town? Nobody will be safe.'

Steve shaped his words slowly and carefully.

'A man has to do what he thinks is right, Mary. These men wouldn't stop if I was to run. They'd come after me. Dawson would make sure of that.'

'You're right, Steve.' Her father looked him straight in the eye as he spoke. 'If every decent lawman ran when trouble comes, this whole territory would be taken over by crooks and killers. There'd be no law and order, no place for ordinary folk.'

'Then at least get word to the nearest federal marshal,' Mary protested. 'These men are all wanted outlaws. Surely the marshal could get some men to help you.'

Steve turned that idea over in his mind for a moment, then shook his head.

'No, Mary, I'm not goin' to back down in the face of

Dawson's threats. This is somethin' I have to do myself.'

'Damn you, Steve. I always though you were as stubborn as a mule. Now I'm sure of it.' There were tears in her eyes as she spoke.

It was just before noon when Mary Marsden entered the small church at the end of the dusty street. It was cool and shadowed inside with the rows of wooden pews opening off on either side of the aisle.

At that time of the morning the church was empty. She went to the front row and knelt down before the statue of the Virgin. Her mind was still in a turmoil. The events of the past two days had been too much for her fragile emotional state.

There had been moments, when she had been kept prisoner inside that shack, when she had feared for her life. When Cal Dawson had thrust her on to his mount in front of him, she had had no idea where he was taking her or what his intentions were.

Being thrust through that cabin doorway with the gun at her head and Cal shouting that he meant to kill her if Steve didn't do exactly as he demanded, had taken her to the edge of real terror. Now there was this new and terrible threat hanging over the man who was to be her husband.

She knew with a sick certainty that he would have to face those six killers alone. No one in town, not even Slim Benson, would dare to stand with him. How could one man possibly go against six of the deadliest gunmen in the territory?

Around her, the silence was absolute. There was not

even a sound from the street outside to mar the utter stillness.

How long she knelt there, struggling to will the gnawing torment in her mind to be still, she didn't know. Here in the peace and tranquillity of the church, time had little meaning.

Mary was not a deeply religious woman, nor did she believe in miracles. Yet now she asked for one, knowing how unlikely it would be for it to be granted.

She remained kneeling for a little while, strangely reluctant to leave the quietude of the church, then rose to her feet and left.

Just as she stepped on to the boardwalk at the end of the narrow path leading from the church she picked out the sound of hoofbeats in the distance. Her first thought was that it might be more of the Double K riders heading back into town, looking for trouble. Then she instantly dismissed that idea. Whoever the rider was, he was coming from the north where the trail led around the tip of the Badlands towards the mountains.

Very few people rode into town from this direction. There was nothing but the wild country there. Almost all of the trails that were used these days ran to the south of Bitter River.

She turned and saw the rider approaching at a slow, leisurely pace. He was a youngish man, sitting tall and loose in the saddle. His hat was pushed on to the back of his head. Twin Colts rested in worn holsters and there was a Winchester strapped across his back.

As he drew nearer she was able to see his face more clearly. A little tremor of apprehension went through her. Somehow, he had the look of a gunhawk about him, hard features and cold eyes.

He reined his mount as he came alongside her. For a instant, his gaze locked with hers. Then he leaned sideways slightly and a faint smile touched his lips.

'Pardon me, ma'am. Is this town Bitter River?'

'Yes.' Mary nodded and tried to keep her voice from faltering. There was an air about this man which, for some reason, disturbed her.

'Could you direct me to the sheriff?'

Mary shaded her eyes and pointed along the street.

'His office is at the far end on the right, almost opposite the hotel.'

'Thank you kindly, ma'am.' Digging in the spurs, he pushed his mount towards the far end of town. Mary watched him go, oddly troubled. The sense of foreboding increased as she saw the stranger rein his mount outside the sheriff's office. Common sense told her that no wanted man would ride into town and deliberately ask for the law. But oddly, she gained little comfort from the thought.

Her instincts told her that, whoever this stranger was, he boded ill for someone.

Slim Benson and Doc Marsden stepped out of the sheriff's office just as the stranger slid from the saddle. He looped the reins around the rail and stepped up easily on to the boardwalk beside them.

'I'm lookin' for the sheriff,' he said quietly. 'Is he around?'

'Not at the moment,' Benson told him. 'I'm his deputy. Is there anythin' I can do for you?'

The stranger shook his head. 'My business is with the sheriff.'

'Then I suggest you try the saloon,' Marsden interposed.

The thin lips twisted into a smile but there was no mirth in it. The stranger turned on his heel and walked in the direction of the doctor's pointing finger. Marsden's gaze followed him closely.

'Ain't seen him around these parts,' he observed. 'I wonder what business he's got with Steve.'

'He weren't wearin' no star,' Benson replied. 'Could be an undercover marshal. From the look o' those guns he certainly knows how to handle 'em.'

Inside the saloon, Steve was standing at the bar, the whiskey in front of him virtually untouched. At that time of day the place was empty. Only the bartender stood behind the counter a few feet away, a smoke dangling from his lips.

The sound of the doors opening brought Steve whirling round, his right hand dropping towards his gun.

The man who stood framed in the doorway bore the unmistakable look of a gunfighter. He held his hands well away from his sides.

'Hold hard there, Sheriff,' he said levelly. 'If I'd come here to kill you, you'd be dead by now.'

Slowly, Steve relaxed but his eyes were still wary. 'You lookin' for me?' he asked.

'That's right.' The man walked up to the bar beside him. Glancing towards the bartender, he said: 'Whiskey.'

He took the makings of a cigarette from his pocket,

rolled it and lit it, inhaling deeply.

'Very well,' Steve said harshly. 'You've found me. Obviously you're a stranger here. What's your business with me?'

The man stared down at his cigarette for a moment. 'I understand there's a man named Clem Dawson in these parts.'

Steve nodded. 'He owns the Double K spread south o' here. You lookin' for work there?'

'Nope. But him an' me have a score to settle. One that goes back a long way. You a friend of his?'

Steve shook his head. 'Not exactly. In fact he's sworn to have me gunned down.'

'That so?' The stranger evinced no surprise at this remark. Instead, he went on quietly: 'Guess that ties in with somethin' I heard along the trail. There's a rumour that the five Kelton brothers are headed this way.'

'You heard right.' Steve gave the other a more penetrating glance. 'You know anythin' about them?'

'Only that they're the meanest bunch of cold-blooded killers around.' The stranger picked up his glass and downed the drink in a single swallow. 'If this *hombre* Dawson has hired them to kill you, I wouldn't give much for your chances.'

'So everybody keeps tellin' me.'

'Seems to me you're in need of a little help, Sheriff.'

Steve eyed the other in surprise. 'You offerin' to be deputized? Why should you want a part in this fight? It ain't got nothin' to do with you. Just who are you? You've got the look of a man who knows how to use those guns. What's your name?'

The stranger gave a tight smile. 'My name ain't important. But my friends call me Denvers. Frank Denvers.'

Steve turned the name over in his mind. Whether or not it was the stranger's real name there was no way of knowing. There were many wanted killers who went under names other than their own. In his drawer in the office there were several posters of men with a reward out for their capture, dead or alive. Perhaps it would be wise for him to run a check on them before accepting this man's unexpected offer of help.

'I'll sure think it over, Denvers,' he said evenly.

'Sure thing, Sheriff. But don't take too long about it. My guess is that time is runnin' out fast.'

'You got something against the Kelton brothers?' Steve asked.

'Never run across 'em in my life,' answered the other quietly. 'But anythin' to do with Dawson I make it my business.' He turned for the door. 'Thanks for the drink, Sheriff. I see you have a hotel here. If you want my help, that's where you'll find me.'

Scarcely had he left than Mary entered. There was a look of undisguised relief on her face.

'That stranger, Steve. What did he want?' Her voice trembled slightly. 'He stopped me just as I came out of church, said he had business with you.'

'I only wish I knew. He says he has a score to settle with Clem Dawson: an old score.'

'So why should he come to you?'

'Let's just say there's somethin' strange about him. He wants to help me finish Dawson.'

'You think he could be a federal marshal?'

Before Steve could answer, the bartender butted in.

'He ain't no marshal, Sheriff. If I were you, I'd watch my back with that *hombre* around.'

Clem Dawson had spent a restless day after leaving town and burying his son in the corner of the grounds near the ranch house. The evening had brought no better edge to his temper. Now, as he sat facing his foreman in the yellow lamplight, the lines around his hard-set mouth deepened.

'Torran and Calder still keepin' a watch on the trail outa town?' he demanded.

Jensen nodded. 'They're still there,' he affirmed. 'You figger Manders will try to leave before that gang gets here?'

Dawson lifted his brows into a straight line.

'What do you think?'

The foreman pursed his lips. 'Ain't no way o' tellin' with a man like him. There's a yeller streak in every man if you can find it.'

Dawson wasn't convinced. Inwardly, he was hoping that the sheriff would stay. His thoughts switched direction abruptly. He drilled Jensen with his eyes.

'There's a job I want you to do for me. That lawyer, Cy Rawlins, could be dangerous if he starts talkin' to the wrong people. He knows too much. I want him out o' the way tonight. Permanently, you understand.'

Jensen grinned. 'Sure thing, boss.'

Dawson held up a hand. 'But I want no trouble with Manders. The Kelton boys will take care of him and, like I told him this mornin', I want him to sweat and keep lookin' over his shoulder all the time.'

'You don't reckon any o' the townfolk will help him when those outlaws ride into town, do you?' There was a faint note of doubt in the foreman's tone. 'There ain't too many in town have any likin' for you.'

Dawson uttered a harsh laugh. 'They may think he's a good sheriff, handy with a gun, but none of 'em will try anythin' with these *hombres*. Guess most folk in Bitter River know their reputation.'

He paused for a moment, then nodded. 'You'd better be on your way. And remember what I said. Stay clear o' Manders. I want him alive when those boys ride into town in a few days.'

Jensen checked his guns, then went out. He went into the courtyard, crossed to the corral, saddled his mount and swung up on to his mount's back.

The lights from the windows only penetrated a little way and soon there was darkness all around him. The sky was clear with a sliver of yellow moon hanging low over the distant hills.

He rode slowly, taking his time, a deep consuming anger inside him. Despite what Dawson had ordered, he had his own intentions for the sheriff. Already, he was turning over various possibilities in his mind.

Twenty minutes later, he approached the river. Stunted bushes grew along the rocky bank and as he drew level with them, two shadowy figures emerged.

'That you, Hal?' called one of the men softly.

He reined his mount as Torran and Calder came out of the shadows.

'I'm ridin' into town to see Rawlins,' he said harshly. 'The boss reckons he's too much of a liability and might talk.'

'You goin' to take care of him?' Calder asked.

'That's right. Could be that the sheriff will be on my tail when I ride back. Just make sure you're ready.'

Torran grinned. 'We'll be ready,' he promised. 'But the boss's orders were to—'

'I know full well what his orders are,' Jensen snapped. 'But I've got a score to settle with that sheriff.'

'Yeah, but . . .' Torran began hesitantly.

'Dawson ain't goin' to know what happens.' Jensen stepped down to tighten the cinch. 'When I come ridin' back from town, Manders will be right behind me. I'll make sure o' that. All you have to do is wait until I give the word.'

'And when the boss hears about it?' Torran sounded dubious.

Jensen's lips curled. 'We won't be here. We ride up to that camp in the hills, pick up the loot, and head south.'

Jensen swung back into the saddle and waited while the two men faded into the darkness on either side of the bridge before riding on.

Once he came within sight of the town, he slowed his mount to a walk. Most of the places were in darkness and there was no one in sight on the street. Lights still showed through the windows of the saloon and there was one in the sheriff's office.

At the very edge of town he dismounted and looped the reins around a post; then he moved into the deep shadows opposite the jail. Here there was a narrow alley which ran beside the hotel. Confident he could not be seen by anyone, he lit a cigarette and settled down to wait.

There was a rising sense of grim amusement in his mind as he visualized how events would shape up if everything went according to the plan he had formulated.

Ten minutes passed and then the light in the sheriff's office was extinguished. A moment later, the door opened and he recognized Manders' tall figure as the sheriff stepped outside. Everything seemed to be going as he had hoped.

He watched keenly as the sheriff stood for a couple of minutes looking up and down the street. Then, as Manders moved along the boardwalk deeper into the town, he moved away to the rear of the hotel.

Here was a large patch of rough, uneven ground. Eyes narrowed, he fought to hold all of the shadows in his attention. Bitter River seemed quiet but it was possible there were other folk abroad. However, he saw nothing out of the ordinary as he made his way quietly along the backs of the houses and stores.

At the far end he found another alley which led in a straight line towards the street. This, he knew, would bring him directly across from the lawyer's office. Moving catlike to the end, he risked a quick look around the corner.

He caught sight of the sheriff immediately. He was standing just outside the saloon, his back to Jensen. Pausing for only a moment, Jensen ran across the street and ducked swiftly into the shadowed doorway.

Silence lay heavily on the street, a deep and brooding silence.

Trying the door handle, he found it was locked. He

had expected this, however, and moved around to the side of the building. There was a window here, its lower edge about three feet from the ground. He took out his knife, slid the blade into the frame and, a moment later, the window was open. Quickly, he pulled himself inside.

Standing quite still to allow his eyes to adjust to the darkness, he made out the vague shapes of a table and a couple of chairs. Silently, he worked his way around them to the far door.

Within a couple of minutes, he was edging his way up the stairs, testing each board beneath his weight. At the top was a short passage with a door leading off on either side.

He eased one of the Colts from its holster, turned the handle of the nearer door, thrust it open and stepped inside. On the bed, Cy Rawlins jerked himself upright as he entered, one hand going towards his pillow.

'Don't try it, Rawlins,' Jensen said softly. 'Now just keep your hands where I can see 'em and move away from that bed.'

'Damn you, Jensen,' Rawlins grated. 'What the hell is this? If Clem Dawson hears about this unwarranted intrusion, he'll—'

Jensen motioned with his gun as the lawyer slid out of bed.

'Dawson sent me here. Seems he thinks you might spill everythin' to the sheriff.'

'Why the hell should I do that?' Rawlins almost choked on his words. 'I'm in this as deep as he is. If he goes down, I go down.'

The foreman drew his lips back over his teeth and

moved forward a couple of paces.

'Reckon he don't see it like that. Now get dressed; you're comin' with me. And hurry unless you want a slug in your belly.'

For a moment, Rawlins seemed on the point of arguing further. But a look at the gun in Jensen's hand dissuaded him. He took up his clothes and struggled into them.

'You won't get away with this,' he muttered.

Jensen waved the Colt menacingly.

'This gun says I will.' He stepped back as Rawlins buttoned up his jacket and thrust his shoes on to his feet. 'Now walk in front of me and no funny moves or I'll kill you right here.'

With the gun prodding him hard between the shoulder blades, Rawlins went down the stairs. At the bottom, Jensen spoke.

'Now get the key and open the door. And not a sound.'

Rawlins did as he was told, turning the key in the lock and opening the door slowly. Keeping the gun on him, Jensen glanced outside, running his gaze along the entire length of the street.

Nothing moved. Then, some twenty yards away, he saw the tall figure of the sheriff emerge from one of the alleys. Manders seemed relaxed, as though confident there would be no trouble that night. Jensen waited as the lawman crossed the street and moved out of sight between the hardware store and the doctor's surgery.

Swiftly, he grabbed the lawyer by the arm and hustled him outside, thrusting him in front of him.

'Keep movin',' he ordered tightly.

'Where are you takin' me?' Rawlins demanded in a low voice. 'Reckon you know the sheriff's doin' his rounds of the town.'

'That's what I'm bankin' on,' Jensen replied.

CHAPTER SIX

GUNSMOKE JUSTICE

Steve paused abruptly at the end of the alley, then turned swiftly. A small sound had reached him from the direction of the street. It had been faint but he felt certain he hadn't imagined it.

He turned and moved back, his eyes drifting from right to left. A sense of unease seized his mind in spite of his efforts to control it. This was a feeling he had experienced on several occasions in the past and he had learned from bitter experience never to doubt it, or ignore it.

Something was wrong but at the moment he couldn't figure out what it was. A second later, he reached the junction where the alley met the street and risked a quick look around. Some thirty yards away were two indistinct figures. In the darkness, it was impossible to identify them.

His first thought was they were a couple of drunks leaving the saloon, for there was something odd about the way they were moving. One was slightly behind the other, his right arm held tightly to his side. Several seconds fled before he realized what was happening. The big man had a gun trained on the other's back and was hustling him along the street.

Drawing his own gun, he stepped out on to the boardwalk.

'Just hold it right there,' he shouted.

At the sound of his voice, the bigger man half-turned. In the light from the saloon he recognized Jensen. The little man suddenly broke free and began running for the far side of the street. It was a foolish thing to do. He had no chance of reaching any cover.

Before Steve could move, a single shot rang out. The running figure staggered in his tracks. Then his knees buckled and he fell face down in the dust.

Swiftly, Steve brought up his own gun.

'Drop your gun, Jensen,' he ordered. 'Or I'll drill you.'

For a split second, the other froze. Then he spun swiftly, loosing off a couple of shots in rapid succession. Instinctively, Steve threw himself back against the boardwalk. The slugs hit the wall immediately behind him, ricocheting away into the distance.

Already, Jensen was running, zigzagging across the street, up on to the boardwalk and into the dark shadows. Steve's shot whined shrilly off the saloon wall. A second shot must have missed its target for the sound of a running horse reached him from the far side of town.

He pushed himself to his feet and ran to the prone

figure. He turned the man over. Already, the sounds had attracted attention. Two figures came out of the saloon and ran over.

'Jensen just shot Rawlins,' Steve said tersely, looking up into the face of the bartender. 'Shot him in the back when he tried to run.'

'Why the hell would he do that?'

'Most likely because Clem Dawson figures he knew too much.'

'Where is the hellion now?' queried the other man.

The fading sound of a horse in the distance answered the question for him. Steve pushed himself upright.

'Take him to the morgue and inform Doc Marsden,' he muttered. 'I'm goin' after Jensen.'

Fortunately, he hadn't corralled his own mount for the night. He pushed the Colt back into its holster and ran along the street. Swiftly, he untied the reins and leapt into the saddle.

Jensen hadn't got too big a lead on him, although in the darkness it was impossible to make out the fleeing gunman. But the sound of hoofbeats told him the killer was still on the trail in front of him, heading in the direction of the Double K ranch.

Now Steve recognized that he was gaining on the other. His own horse was fresh whereas Jensen must have ridden all the way from the spread into town.

Up ahead of him was the river which marked the northern boundary of Dawson's spread. He knew he had to make a quick decision. Once across the river there could be more of Dawson's hands lying in wait in the shadows. Moments later, the decision was made for him.

As he reined up his mount he realized he could no longer hear the hoofbeats of Jensen's horse. He edged his own to the side of the trail and slid noiselessly from the saddle.

Crouching down, he went forward on foot, pushing his vision into the enshrouding darkness, searching for any sign of movement. There was nothing, only the sound of the rushing water broke the stillness.

On reaching the end of the bridge, he waited tensely for a full two minutes, then eased himself upright. He knew Jensen was somewhere close by, waiting for him to show himself. Then he picked out the soft snicker of a horse over to his left on the other side of the river.

Edging sideways, he lowered himself down the steep, rocky riverbank, making no noise. He was figuring on Jensen expecting him to ride over the bridge into an ambush. Moving through the water, he made it to the other side.

He crouched there for a moment, listening intently. Then, bracing himself, he crawled up the far bank, his gun ready. The darkness was suddenly pierced a split second later by the brief glare of gunfire. The bullet smashed into the stonework of the bridge less than a foot from his head.

Instinctive reflex took over. Swiftly, he hurled himself forward and down, rolling sideways as the second shot came, but this time it was from a slightly different direction.

Steve thought fast. Either Jensen had shifted his position or there were two gunmen out there and he had been led into an ambush. Inwardly, he cursed himself for not recalling that Dawson had told him that every trail out of Bitter River would be watched.

'You'll never get out o' this alive, Manders.' The harsh voice rang out from the darkness ahead. 'Reckon you're finished this time.'

Trying to gauge where the voice had come from, he realized it hadn't been Jensen's. Keeping his head down, he felt about him. His fingers touched a large stone near his foot. He knew the others weren't exactly sure where he was and it was just as difficult for them to pick him out as it was for him to locate them.

He clutched the stone in his fingers, then tossed it swiftly towards the opposite side of the bridge. It struck with a low clatter, followed instantly by a spurt of gunfire.

Swiftly, he brought up his Colt and fired at the man's position. There was a loud gasp of agony and he knew the shot had gone home. Whether the man was dead or only wounded, it was impossible to tell but he heard no sound of movement.

He waited for only a moment, then got his legs under him and darted forward, throwing himself into a rocky hollow just as a slug hummed past him. Now he could just make out the shape of the man he'd shot.

The other lay slumped forward over the rim of a shallow depression. One glance was sufficient to tell him the man was dead. His gun lay a few inches from his outflung hand. The man's face was just visible.

Steve had expected it to be Jensen but he soon saw he had been mistaken. It was Herb Torran who lay there, eyes staring sightlessly at the stars.

A soft movement from the bushes a short distance away alerted him to the fact that there was still another to be taken care of, almost certainly Jensen. He waited tensely for the man to make his move. When it came, it almost took him off his guard.

The dark shape rose up less than three feet away. Steve glimpsed the grin on the man's face as he levelled his gun on him. Without thinking, he thrust himself back down the slope, twisting his body so that he was partially shielded by the dead man beside him.

The gun in the man's hand roared and the slug tore into the rock near Steve's head, kicking up splinters of rock. In almost the same moment, his own gun spoke. Dimly, he saw the other jerk back, then reel sideways on his heels under the impact of lead in his body. He stood swaying, struggling to maintain enough hold on life to squeeze off another shot.

Before he could do so, his legs gave under him and he pitched forward on to his face. Steve let his breath go in a harsh gasp and got unsteadily to his feet. Prodding the body in front of him with his foot, he knew by the limp way the man flopped on to his side that he was dead.

Steve holstered his guns and moved back towards the bridge where his mount stood waiting. What instinct warned him of a third man's presence, he didn't know. Some of the tension had left him but there was still enough to give a hint of danger a second before he glimpsed the sudden movement out of the corner of his eye.

His hands dropped towards his guns as he made to turn.

'Go ahead, Manders, make your play.' Jensen's voice reached him out of the darkness just behind him.

There was a note of triumph in the big foreman's tone. 'You'll never reach your guns before I put a bullet into your hide.'

'You goin' to shoot me in the back like the low-down polecat you are?'

Jensen uttered a dry laugh. 'Oh, I'm goin' to do that, make no mistake. Dawson wants you alive so those outlaws can take care of you. But I've got other ideas.'

'And you reckon Dawson will believe anythin' you tell him? You're foolin' yourself.'

'So you say. Dawson don't matter. I don't aim to go back there and work for a pittance. With Torran and Calder now conveniently out o' the way, I reckon all that loot from the bank hold-up is mine.'

'Ain't you forgettin' Cy Rawlins and Seb Butler?'

Steve knew he was merely playing for time, waiting for a moment to catch the other off guard. With two guns lined on him, he didn't have much of a chance if he made a play for his own.

Tensing himself, he tried to estimate exactly where the other was, knowing that if he did take a chance, he couldn't afford to miss.

'This is where you get it, Manders. I've been itchin' to do this ever since you showed me up in the saloon.'

Steve detected the abrupt change in the foreman's voice, knew that the other's fingers were tightening on the triggers.

Before he could move, the shot came, tearing the silence into fragments. He flinched involuntarily. Several seconds passed before he realized he was still alive. Dumbfounded, he swung round. Jensen was already on his knees, his body folding on itself. One of his guns went off, the bullet ploughing into the soil in front of him.

'Reckon it was a good thing I decided to follow you from town, Sheriff.'

Whirling, Steve saw the tall figure coming towards him, a Winchester in his hand. He swallowed hard.

'Reckon you saved my life,' he said.

The other eased the rifle back across his shoulders and stood for a moment, staring down at the three bodies beside the trail.

'At least, you got two of the coyotes,' he remarked drily. 'You know these *hombres*?'

'Yeah, I know 'em all. Three of Dawson's hired gunslingers. This one's been nursin' a grievance ever since I knocked him out in the saloon.'

'What was all that about a bank hold-up?'

'These critters held up the bank a few days back. I reckon they've stashed the money somewhere safe.'

Together they walked to where their horses stood waiting. Steve glanced sideways at his companion.

'How did you know there'd be trouble like this?' he asked.

In the dimness, he saw the flash of teeth as the other grinned.

'I spotted someone from my window, movin' around the back of the hotel. Seemed to me he had somethin' on his mind and didn't want to be seen. I figgered he was up to no good so I decided to follow him.'

Steve nodded. 'Dawson must've ordered him to get rid of Cy Rawlins and he took it into his head to pay me back at the same time.'

'Sure looks that way,' Denvers agreed. He swung up

into the saddle and together they rode back into town.

Fifty miles to the south, five men sat their mounts among a group of hump-backed hills. To the north of them lay the Badlands, a region of scrub and alkali that was hell to cross. In that wide desert area there were no trails to follow and precious little water.

For three days they had ridden hard across the wide grasslands, moving cautiously and deliberately avoiding any homesteads and ranches on the way. Men with a price on their heads and the promise of money at the end of the trail, they had no intention of advertising their presence in the territory.

The man who sat in the saddle, a little away from the others, was Brett Kelton. He had a rocklike face, scarred by many brutal battles in the past. He glanced back at the others. 'You sure this rancher can be trusted, Matt?'

Grinning wolfishly, Matt Kelton, three years younger than Brett, the eldest of the five, nodded.

'He seemed mighty anxious to get rid o' this sheriff, Brett. And ten thousand dollars for a few minutes work ain't to be passed over.'

Ed Kelton slid from his mount and gave a non-committal grunt.

'I say we should've found out a bit more about him. For all we know he could be lurin' us into a trap. Don't forget there's plenty o' reward money out for all of us. Mebbe he's hopin' to collect that.'

He threw an apprehensive glance at the sky. Close to the horizon, dense black thunderheads were gathering, blotting out the stars and promising a storm. 'Reckon we'd better find shelter for the night.'

Brett gave a nod. He cast an appraising look around him and jerked a thumb to his left.

'Yonder,' he muttered tersely. 'Looks like an old Indian trail leadin' into those trees.'

Ed remounted and they turned their mounts to the upgrade. Around them, the smell of the night was a blend of sunbaked rock and the bitter dust from the Badlands.

The rain began just as they entered the trees, tall firs that would provide them with a shield against the worst of the coming downpour. Brett led the way, following the trail for half a mile, cursing as low branches slashed across his head.

Here, they came upon a small clearing. Leaving their mounts to graze on the tough, wiry grass, they built a small fire in the middle. Among the firs, they were sufficiently far from the trail to escape any prying eyes that might be in the vicinity.

They had seen no one during the past two days but men on the run from the law took no chances. Lightning suddenly sheeted across the heavens with an eye-searing brilliance. The darkness grew more intense as the thunder rolled above the trees.

Brett took some dried beef from his saddle-bag and thrust the long strips into his mouth. He chewed on them reflectively as he sat there, feeling the warmth from the fire settling deep into his body. When he had finished, he stared across the leaping flames at Matt.

'This man who gave you the message from Dawson.

You're sure of him?'

'Of course I'm sure of him. He was no lawman or federal marshal.'

'Let's hope you're right, otherwise we might have to fight our way outa this town.'

Butting in, Seth muttered: 'What do you know about this sheriff?'

'Nothin' much. Fast with a gun, so they reckon. And if he's been warned we're comin', he might have a few tricks up his sleeve.'

Brett's grin was like an animal's in the firelight.

'I reckon if Dawson's given him warnin', there ain't nobody in town who'll stand with him. That makes it five against one. Pretty good odds I'd say.' He threw another glance at his younger brother. 'You got somethin' on your mind, Matt?'

'Just somethin' Dawson's hired hand told me when we met.'

Brett's expression hardened.

'What was that?' he demanded roughly.

'Seems this rancher Dawson ain't quite sure we can take this lawman by ourselves. He's also sent word to the Nangordo Kid.'

'He's what?' Seth Kelton jerked up his head in surprise, his lips drawn back across his teeth. 'Reckon he's got some bad information. Last I heard, the Nangordo Kid was holed up in the hills north o' Abilene with a posse on his tail.'

Frank stirred the edge of the fire with his foot, sending red sparks high into the air. He laughed harshly; a hard, mirthless sound in the flickering fireglow.

'Reckon we'll show this rancher we're more'n

enough without bringin' in that hellcat.'

Brett put an end to any further conversation.

'All right,' he said. 'Now I reckon we'd better get some sleep. I ain't lookin' forward to ridin' across those Badlands tomorrow.'

He rolled himself in his blankets and stretched himself out on the grass a few feet from the fire, resting his head on his saddle. Before closing his eyes, he ordered: 'Seth, you take the first watch and then Frank.'

'Why the hell do we need to keep watch?' Seth said angrily. 'There ain't a livin' thing within twenty miles of here apart from a few coyotes and rattlers.'

'Just do as I say.'

Still grumbling, Seth moved off into the trees, hitching up his gunbelt around his waist. Already, rain was beginning to drip from the branches overhead and more vivid lightning strokes flashed in the near distance.

At first light, they ate a hurried meal, then threw dirt on to the fire and rode out. The storm had moved away some time during the latter half of the night. Already, the eastern horizon showed redly through the trees as the dawn brightened.

Brett Kelton eyed the coming dawn apprehensively. Inwardly, he had hoped the day would remain cloudy. They had filled their canteens from a small stream which gushed down from the higher levels of the hills but even this precaution might not be enough in the blistering heat of day on the alkali flats between them and their destination.

Three hours before high noon, they came out of the

sheltering trees and there in front of them lay the Badlands. Forty miles of hell to be crossed, and he knew they'd still be only half-way across it by nightfall.

The alkali was treacherous, more so than sand. In parts it was almost as hard as rock, yet in others it was soft and shifting, their mounts sinking into it almost up to their knees. Plenty of men had died out there, leaving only their bones bleaching in the sun.

He'd have preferred to skirt around it to the west but that would have more than doubled their journey. It would also have increased the risk of them being seen and recognized. There were plenty of wanted posters with their faces on them in this part of the territory. Somehow, he doubted if any man in his right mind would venture across the region which lay spread out in front of them.

The blazing sun threw numberless small shadows across the flats as they urged their mounts forward. Out of the shade of the trees, the scorching sunlight was an agony that beat like a fist on their backs and shoulders. Sweat began to drip from their foreheads into their eyes.

All around them, the harsh, glaring sunlight was reflected from the white alkali. Above their heads, the sky was a cloudless, burnt-out blue. Nowhere was there any shade and the only moving things they saw were the sidewinders and scorpions.

Very soon they were all drooping listlessly in the saddle. Their lips were parched and cracked and the tiny sips of water Brett allowed them to take from their canteens brought them no refreshment.

Matt pushed himself up in the saddle.

'Why the hell did we have to take this trail?' he grated harshly.

A little way in the lead, Brett swung on him.

'Because it's the only way to Bitter River. You want some o' that money this rancher is payin' us, don't yuh?'

'If we don't find some place outa this goddamn sun, reckon we won't make it to Bitter River to claim it,' Matt retorted.

Throughout the long afternoon, they rode north. By slow degrees, their shadows lengthened. By the time the sun set they could barely sit in the saddle. But greed drove them on. At last, just as twilight was deepening into night, Brett called a halt. Wearily, they slid from the saddle. The day's heat, trapped in the alkali, seeped through their boots but around them, the temperature was falling rapidly.

It was not the best of places to make camp but they had no other choice. There was also nothing with which they could make a fire, nor would Brett have allowed it even if the makings were there. The chances of anyone riding the Badlands at night were virtually zero. But out here, a fire could be spotted from miles away.

They rolled themselves in their blankets and settled down for the night. This time, Brett gave no orders for a look-out to be posted. They were all bone-weary and saddle-worn after the long, gruelling day. Within minutes, all of them, with the exception of Matt, were asleep.

He had the feeling there was something mighty strange about this job they had been offered. It was a feeling that had gnawed at him ever since the night he had met the stranger in a bar in Cranton's Bend. Somehow, when he had put the proposition to him, the man seemed to know who he was.

The offer was $10,000 if he would get his brothers together, ride into some town called Bitter River and gun down the sheriff. The thought had occurred to Matt that it might be a trap and they would ride in to find a federal marshal and more than a score of men waiting for them.

Even when the man had given him $2,000 with the promise of the rest when the job was done, it had not erased his suspicions completely. He knew that Brett had figured it might be a trap from the beginning.

Ed, Seth and Frank were just born killers, fast with their guns but not with their heads. They would go wherever Brett led them.

He, however, had a plan. If this was some plot to lure them into an ambush in this town, their first visit should be to the Double K ranch to check on this *hombre* Dawson. Not until they had satisfied themselves that he had a damned good reason for wanting this sheriff out of the way in this fashion, would he agree to ride on into the town.

With these thoughts running through his mind, he rolled over and fell asleep.

Clem Dawson had spent the night sitting in his chair in front of the fire. He had slept only in brief snatches and this had brought a vicious edge to his temper. The previous day he'd received the news that Rawlins was dead, that Hal Jensen had carried out his orders in that respect. But the news that not only Jensen, but Calder and Torran, had been found shot near the river had both shocked and stunned him.

How the hell had that happened? And who had done it was a mystery he couldn't figure out. If it had been Manders who had trailed Jensen out of town, by rights the sheriff should also be dead by now. One man against three were pretty good odds for his men and it would have been simple for at least one of his boys to drop the sheriff from cover.

If Manders took it into his head to ride out and take him in on a charge of conspiracy, he doubted if any of the men he had left on the ranch would do anything to stop it. None of them was a gunman like those three who had been killed.

Pacing up and down the room, he wondered where those five gunhawks were. If he had them at his back, he'd feel perfectly safe no matter what the sheriff had up his sleeve.

Callan, the man he had sent to Cranton's Bend, had been convinced they would turn up. But from what he knew they had sixty miles to ride before they reached Bitter River and a lot could happen on the way, especially if they decided to cross the Flats.

Going out into the courtyard, he called across to Callan.

'I'm expectin' those men you met, Jeff. Seems they may have had trouble on the way. To my way o' thinking, they should be here by now.'

'You want me to ride out and take a look-see, boss?'

Dawson gave a nod. 'Reckon that might be best.

'You know which way they'll be comin'?'

'My guess is they'll cross the Badlands instead o' making their way by any other trail. If there ain't been any trouble, they shouldn't be more'n a dozen miles away.' Grimly he added: 'Hurry them along.'

CHAPTER SEVEN

HELLRIDERS

The second day crossing the flats was even worse than the first. Brett Kelton tried to push his mount faster but the animal was at the limit of its endurance. Head down, it trod the blistering alkali at a slow pace and no amount of urging would make it increase its gait.

There was no respite from the sun which was a blazing disc in the heavens. A few hump-backed ridges poked out of the ground but none was high enough to provide any shade. Even through closed lids, the glare spiked redly into their brains.

Seth licked his caked lips.

'Hell, that information you got from that fella had better be right, Matt,' he mumbled. 'I'm reckonin' even ten thousand dollars ain't worth this hell.'

'Ain't nothin' we can do about it now,' Matt replied, screwing up his eyes to search the featureless, heat-shimmering horizon. 'Too late to turn back. We'd never make it that way.'

At the rear of the bunch, Frank Kelton sat slumped in the saddle, his shoulders hunched forward over the drooping back of his horse. The youngest of the five, he had been against this plan from the beginning. Now, he was regretting joining up with his brothers.

The heat made the throbbing agony in his head more difficult to bear. Holding up the occasional stage or bank was one thing but this was something he hadn't bargained for when he had agreed to ride with the others.

Sweat dripped continually down his forehead and into his eyes and he lacked the strength to wipe it away. At times, he found himself slipping lower and lower in the saddle.

Mile after endless mile, the glaring whiteness stretched in front of them. It was a vast wilderness in which nothing moved but the occasional rattler slithering across the ground at their approach.

An hour after noon, Brett held up his hand and called a halt. It was clear the horses could not go much further without a rest. Their only food since entering these Badlands had been a few tufts of coarse grass which somehow managed to survive in the arid earth.

Their water was almost finished and he knew that unless they found more before nightfall, they were in a heap of trouble. Even the small sips they now allowed themselves seemed to soak into their swollen tongues and parched throats and little went down into their stomachs.

'What do you figger on doin' once we hit this town?' Ed asked. He had difficulty getting the words out.

Brett scratched the stubble on his chin where the grains of alkali had rubbed the flesh raw.

'First we find someplace where we can hide out,' he growled. 'I still got my suspicions about this rancher, Dawson. Until we're plumb sure of him, we stay away from the town. Just in case this *hombre* has his eye on the reward money out for us.'

'Reckon that makes sense.' Frank agreed.

'If there's no federal marshal lyin' in wait for us in the town and Dawson is on the level, then I guess we do what he wants. Ride into town and rid him o' this sheriff.'

'And the Nangordo Kid? He might have some ideas of his own.'

Brett forced a grin that was more like a grimace.

'Guess we'll have to do the job afore he does. That way, he won't have any claim on this ten thousand dollars.' He pulled his hatbrim down a little further to shade his eyes. 'I don't aim to share that money with any other hired gunslinger. Reckon I'll make sure Dawson knows that afore we do anythin'.'

Now that the Nangordo Kid's name had been brought up, a fresh thought struck him. It was one he didn't like. Maybe this rancher was a lot more cunning than he had thought.

He and his brothers were more than enough to gun down one man. So why had Dawson also sent for this gunhawk? Either this sheriff was lightning with a gun and he figured he might need a back-up – or he was planning to sell out them, and the Kid, to the law.

He voiced his thoughts to the others. Matt took off his hat and fanned his head.

'If he's plannin' that, Brett, he's as good as dead,' he muttered.

Nodding, Brett threw a squinting glance at the sun.

'We'd better get movin' again afore we fry in this hellhole.'

He raked spurs across his mount's flanks. The others did likewise, struggling to stay upright in the saddle.

For a further two hours they headed north. Then, abruptly, Seth uttered a croaking shout and pointed.

'What is it?' Brett followed the direction of his brother's pointing finger.

At first he could make out nothing in the shimmering heat-curtain. Then he spotted the blurred outline in the distance.

The lone rider was still about a mile away but, whoever he was, he'd obviously seen them and was heading in their direction.

'Trouble?' Matt muttered, his right hand hovering close to the gun at his waist.

'Could be.'

'Reckon he'd be a fool to tangle with the five of us.' Frank moved his mount forward until the brothers were strung out across the alkali.

They reined up and waited.

The rider was moving quickly, his mount kicking up the white dust beneath its feet. He halted a couple of yards in front of them.

'Guess you're the men Clem Dawson is expectin',' he said, his gaze flicking from one to the other. If he felt any surprise at seeing the kind of men they were, none showed on his face.

'That's right,' Brett said.

'This is the *hombre* I met in Cranton's Bend,' Matt said.

Brett scrutinized the man closely, noticing the way he held himself tautly in the saddle, and the pearl-handled Colts in their holsters. It was evident the other was no gunman.

'He sent me to look for you. Three of our boys were killed a little while back. He reckons it were the sheriff did it.'

Brett's brows met in a hard line above his narrowed eyes.

'Seems to me this sheriff is mighty handy with a gun.'

The other nodded. 'Guess so. He also killed Clem Dawson's son. Now Clem is determined to make Sheriff Manders sweat before he dies.'

'You got any water on you?' Matt demanded roughly.

'Sure.' Callan handed over his canteen and waited as they passed it among themselves, swilling the water around their mouths before swallowing it.

'All right.' Brett handed the canteen back. 'You'd better take us to this boss o' yours. And everythin' had better be on the level or there'll be more dead men lyin' around.'

Steve Manders woke with the knowledge that something had been niggling at the back of his mind just before he had fallen asleep. He lay for a moment before thoughts and memory began to come back into his mind. He had been up most of the previous night following the shoot-out with Hal Jensen and the two Double K gunmen.

Having had three hours' sleep, he drew in several

deep breaths and felt his head clear a little. It was now late afternoon. Outside the sun was still bright and most of the town seemed to be going about its business as normal.

Dousing his face in cold water, he found himself thinking over the little idea he'd had earlier. That ambush had clearly been planned to kill him and now he had the impression that there had been more behind Jensen's determination to get even with him for the beating the foreman had received.

Little pieces of the puzzle were now slotting into place. Cy Rawlins being shot down in the street. Old Seb Butler's testimony. Only the money being taken from the bank safe and the rich haul of gold being left. Certainly not the hallmark of the usual run of outlaws.

But it would take more than that to convince Clem Dawson and most of the townsfolk that Cal had been the brains behind that hold-up. With all four members of the gang now dead there was no way of getting the truth out of them.

The only way he could do it, to give these people the proof they wanted, was to find where that haul had been stashed. Inwardly, he cursed himself for not having thought of the most obvious place earlier.

A place which Cal Dawson had believed was known only to himself. That old mining-camp up in the hills.

The more he thought about it, the more logical it seemed.

He pulled on his jacket, buckled the gunbelt about his waist and went out into the street.

He found Slim Benson in the office. Immediately he noticed the odd expression on the deputy's face.

'Somethin' wrong, Slim?' he asked.

'I'm . . . I'm really sorry about this, sheriff, but I . . .' He paused, then reached up and took the badge from his shirt and laid it on the desk in front of Steve. 'It's just that I have a wife and two kids, as you know, and with these hired killers ridin' into town any day now, I . . .'

'I guess I understand, Slim. This ain't your fight. It's me these killers want.'

'You're goin' to stay here and let them come?'

'I guess so. I sure ain't goin' to turn tail and run like most of the townsfolk think. No tellin' when they'll ride into town but first there's somethin' I have to do.'

'What's that?'

'I reckon I've figgered out where Cal Dawson and those others hid that money they took from the bank. If it's where I think it is, then that'll nail those four killers to the robbery.'

'You need someone to accompany you, Sheriff?'

Steve whirled swiftly. Denvers was leaning nonchalantly against the street door, rolling a cigarette in his fingers.

'Couldn't help overhearing,' Denvers said casually. 'Seems you just lost a deputy. Like I said in the saloon, my offer still stands.'

Steve thought fast. This man was a stranger. He knew nothing about him or his past. There was no doubt he knew how to use his guns and he didn't seem like a man who would back down in the face of danger.

Yet how far could he trust him? he wondered. And what was his motive for offering this help?

'You said you had an old score to settle with Clem

Dawson,' he said eventually. 'Mind tellin' me what it is?'

Denvers drew deeply on his cigarette, blew smoke into the air.

'Guess there ain't no reason why you shouldn't know, Sheriff. Seeing as you're the law around these parts.' He stepped into the office and closed the door quietly. 'Mebbe you don't know how Dawson got the money to buy that spread. Well, I'll tell you. Back in the war, he headed a gang that held up Army wagons from the North, took the guns and sold 'em to the Confederates.'

Steve leaned back in his chair.

'I've heard rumours to that effect,' he said. 'But only rumours.'

Denvers shook his head. His face was suddenly hard, brows drawn together.

'Ain't no rumour. My brother was in the army at that time. He was one o' the men ridin' with those wagons. Dawson and his band ambushed this wagon, killed most o' the men ridin' with it. My brother and three others were captured, taken into the rocks, and shot down in cold blood.'

Steve had met too many men who'd lied to him when questioned not to know that this man was telling the truth.

'I get the picture,' he said thinly. 'Guess you've got a right to want to see Dawson swingin' on the end of a rope.'

Denvers' smile held the promise of death in it.

'I just want to see him at the wrong end of my gun,' he gritted. 'If I'm on the side o' the law when I shoot him down like the no-good snake that he is, I'll be satisfied.'

'All right.' Steve reached a sudden decision. He bent forward, took the star which Benson had placed on the table and pinned it on to Denver's shirt. 'I'm swearin' you in as my deputy.'

Five minutes later, they both rode out of town, turning on to the trail leading up into the hills. Steve noticed that his companion still had the Winchester strapped across his back. Momentarily, he wondered what would happen if Denvers caught up with Clem Dawson. Somehow, he doubted whether the rancher would walk away from the encounter.

There was a deep bitterness gnawing away at Denvers, one which would never be erased until the rancher was dead.

By the time they reached the deep ravine cutting into the hillside, the sun was lowering towards the west. Long shadows lay across the ground in front of the shack. Stepping from the saddle, Steve led the way inside.

Standing in the doorway, Denvers threw a swift glance around.

'I don't reckon it's goin' to be easy finding that money if it's here,' he remarked sombrely. 'There are a helluva lot of places where it could be hidden. And this *hombre* Cal Dawson would've made mighty sure it wouldn't be found by anyone happenin' on this place by accident.'

Steve shrugged. 'We still have a few hours o' daylight left. Let's start lookin'.'

'There are a couple of shafts yonder.' Denvers pointed. 'I'll check them.'

He walked over and examined the splintered

wooden planks which covered the shafts. Five minutes later, he came back.

'Nothin' there,' he said. 'They seemed a likely place. Hang the bags with rope from the boards and nobody would think of lookin' there.'

'Then it must be somewhere inside,' Steve responded.

His glance swept the large room. It was littered with rubbish. On the floor were several empty cartridge-cases where the Double K men had fired on the posse just before he had shot Cal.

There was a long table, a few chairs and several iron bunks set around the walls. Over in one corner were pickaxes and shovels, all rusted.

Without turning, Steve said: 'There's another room yonder. You'd better search that. I'll look around in here.'

Denvers went through the door and Steve heard him moving around, searching through the debris.

He turned his attention to the bunks. Some were covered with bedding which was now mildewed and covered with dust. Nowhere was there any sign of a bag. Then he tested the floorboards, feeling around them with his fingers for any which were loose. All of them, however, appeared to be in good condition and there was no evidence of any of them being recently prised up.

Not until he had eliminated most of the logical places did he happen to glance at the large stove near the wall. Bending, he lifted the heavy iron top and glanced inside. A few moments later, he had withdrawn the two bags just as Denvers came back.

'Looks like we just struck gold,' Steve said drily. 'The sooner we get this back to the bank, the better. The ain't no doubt now as to the identity o' those four robbers.'

'Seems they intended comin' back for them some time.'

'It explains why Jensen was so desperate to kill me even though it went against Clem Dawson's orders. He never meant to return to the ranch. Once he got me out o' the way, he figgered on ridin' up here, picking this up, and headin' for the border. If I hadn't shot those two others, he'd have killed them himself.'

Clem Dawson was at the window when he saw the five men ride into the courtyard with Jeff. A wave of relief swept over him as he gave the men a swift appraisal. Even though he knew of them only by reputation, it was clear he had made the right choice in hiring them.

So far, there had been no word from the Nangordo Kid but there was still time for him to arrive. He did not intend sending these men into town for a few more days. The longer time went on, the more sleepless nights Manders would have, wondering when his time had come.

The thought gave him immense satisfaction, knowing that nothing could stop this revenge for the death of his son, and the timing of it rested with him alone. He had but to say the word and Manders was finished.

He opened the door and stepped out on to the veranda. A little warning voice at the back of his mind told him that these men were killers who followed no law but their own. He would have to play this carefully.

'Welcome to the Double K, boys,' he called loudly. Noticing the white alkali dust that smeared their faces and clothing, he knew he'd been right about the trail they had followed. 'Leave your mounts there. They'll be taken care of.'

'You Dawson?' grunted the big man who came striding across the courtyard.

'That's right. Clem Dawson. I own this spread.'

'Reckon you know who we are.' Brett inclined his head towards his brothers. 'You say there's a job needin' to be done and you're willin' to pay well.'

Dawson gave a nod. He gestured towards the house.

'Reckon we'd best talk inside. You all look as if you need some grub and somethin' to wash that alkali dust outa your throats.'

Without answering, Brett followed Dawson into the house, gesturing to the other four to follow.

'Sit yourselves down, boys.' Dawson indicated the chairs around the big table. 'I'll get some food rustled up for you and somethin' to drink.'

In spite of the fact that he'd sent for these men and agreed to pay them well, Dawson felt uneasy in their presence. At the moment, he was wishing he'd just sent for the Nangordo Kid. One man would have been much easier to control than these five.

Once they had eaten their fill and were seated with glasses and a couple of bottles of whiskey in front of them, Brett leaned his elbows on the table and spoke.

'You sure you got the rest o' that ten thousand dollars?'

'You can rest assured you'll get the sum we agreed.' Dawson forced calmness into his voice. With there being little trust on both sides, he knew he was walking a thin line where these men were concerned.

From further along the table, Matt said tightly:

'We'd like to see the colour o' those bills before we sit down to any serious talkin'.'

Dawson stiffened. He knew he had no guarantee that these men wouldn't kill him and simply take the money. He ran his tongue nervously around his lips. Then he got heavily to his feet and walked over to the small safe. He twisted the lock of the combination and pulled the door open.

He took out the wad of dollar bills, carried it to the table and set it down in front of them.

'Yours,' he said tautly, 'once this job is finished.'

It was impossible for him to miss the look on their faces and the greed in their eyes as they stared down at the money.

'Reckon we could just—' Frank muttered.

'Hold your tongue,' Brett said fiercely. He sat back in his chair. 'You seem to be on the level, Dawson. None of us has any likin' for the law and from what we've heard, you ain't either.'

'You're damned right I ain't,' Dawson replied, a deep anger in his tone. 'My son is lyin' out yonder, six feet under. Manders did that. He also killed three o' my best men. There ain't no way he's gettin' away with that.'

Brett grinned. 'So now we have to decide how and when we do it.'

'He sweats it out for a little while yet,' Dawson responded tersely. 'I want him to suffer.'

'Best if we wait until he rides outa town and cut him down from ambush,' Seth suggested.

'No!' Dawson almost shouted the denial. 'It's got to be in town where everybody can see what happens to anybody who opposes me.'

Brett pursed his lips into a hard line. His eyes glinted dangerously.

'If this *hombre* is as fast with a gun as you say, one or two of us could get hit.'

'Five men against one.' Dawson tried to keep the sarcasm out of his voice. 'Anyways, there are plenty o' places in town where a couple o' men could conceal themselves. I ain't got anythin' against him bein' shot in the back.'

Matt Kelton grinned wolfishly. 'And how can we be sure none o' the townsfolk won't side with him when the showdown comes?'

'That's already been taken care of,' Dawson assured him. 'I've spread word around Bitter River that you're comin' with the Nangordo Kid. Even the deputy has quit.' He shook his head emphatically. 'Ain't nothin' so sure as the fact that he'll have to face you alone.'

Seth's eyes narrowed a shade. 'You're tellin' us that the whole o' Bitter River knows we're here?' His tone was hard and held a brittle edge.

Dawson immediately went on the defensive.

'Weren't no other way to make sure nobody backed the sheriff in this.' He felt suddenly apprehensive and vulnerable.

'So what's to stop somebody ridin' outa town and runnin' hell for leather to the nearest marshal?'

That thought hadn't occurred to Dawson and he knew he had to think fast.

'Not a chance,' he said at last. 'I got every trail outa

town covered just to make sure the sheriff don't try to leave before I've finished with him. The entire town is bottled up so tight not even a rat could get out without me knowin' about it.'

'You'd better be damn sure about that,' Brett replied. 'But I aim to make certain.'

Dawson moved across the room and replaced the money in the safe.

'What exactly do you intend to do?' he enquired sharply.

'Once me and the boys find a place to hide out, I'm takin' Frank with me into town. Just to satisfy ourselves there ain't no surprises waitin' for us when we do ride in. And to check out a couple of suitable places where two of us can get the drop on Manders if things don't go to plan.'

Dawson drew in a deep breath.

'Just so long as you ain't seen. I don't want any shoot-out until I give the word.'

Brett uttered a loud laugh.

'When you've been on the run from the law as long as we have, you soon learn not to take any chances.'

Dawson eyed each man in turn.

'There are plenty o' beds in the bunkhouse where you can stay. I can—'

'We'll find us a place in the hills,' Brett interrupted. 'Stayin' here would be too risky. Might be that sheriff could ride out here. If he was killed on your spread, you'd have a whole heap o' explainin' to do.' There was a sly expression on his face as he added: 'And I guess you wouldn't want that.'

'No,' Dawson conceded. 'The less folk know about

my business, the better.'

'One of us will ride here every day until you give the word.'

Dawson thought better than to argue. He nodded in acceptance.

'I'll see you have plenty of food and drink to take with you.'

After they had ridden off, he went back into the house, his mind filled with troubled thoughts. The deep, burning anger inside him over Cal's death was still as fierce as ever. But there was now a nagging little suspicion that he might have bought himself a lot of trouble by hiring these gunhawks.

He knew he hadn't the guts to face down the sheriff himself in a gunfight. But he had made his decision. Now he would have to live with it and hope it turned out as he'd planned.

CHAPTER EIGHT

NIGHT PROWLERS

An hour before nightfall, the five Kelton brothers had found themselves a small cave that cut back for some twelve feet into a ridge of rock about three miles from the Double K ranch. Here there was room enough for all of them and a space in which to light a fire. As they squatted around it, Ed doled out some of the food Dawson had given them. There was also water and six bottles of whiskey.

Outside, the horses whinnied softly in the deepening dusk.

'Reckon there'll be no chance of anyone findin' us here, Brett,' Frank muttered. He took a swallow of the raw spirit, grimaced as it hit the back of his throat. He wiped his mouth with the back of his hand. 'You serious about goin' into town tonight?' he asked. 'Could be a mite dangerous, especially if that sheriff is on the prowl.'

'Hell, he's got to sleep sometime. And if the deputy

has quit, there won't be anybody left.'

'I reckon if we do spot him, we should kill him right there. Save us a whole heap o' trouble.'

'No.' Brett rasped the word. Inwardly, he wasn't sure why he intended to go through with this exactly as Dawson wanted. Honour among killers, perhaps, he thought wryly. And, somehow, the idea of a showdown with the law appealed to him.

There had been sheriffs and federal marshals on his trail for years and they hadn't caught up with him yet. Always, he and his brothers had remained one step ahead of the law across half a dozen states. That was the way he intended it should stay.

Beyond the mouth of the cave the sky was darkening and there was a bank of clouds building up towards the north-west. He rolled a smoke, went out and stood staring up at the sky. There would be little moonlight and he didn't envisage any problems getting in and out of town unnoticed.

Most of the folk would be asleep by the time he and Frank rode in. Maybe a few early-morning revellers leaving the saloons. And there was always the possibility this lawman made a round of the town before turning in. Frank came out to stand beside him.

'When do we ride, Brett?'

'When I say so. We wait until everybody's off the streets. Most o' the folk will be waitin' for somethin' to happen and there could be eyes watching everywhere.'

Somewhere in the distance, a coyote howled. It was a mournful, dismal sound that was echoed a few moments later from a different direction.

Two hours passed, then three. At last, Brett decided.

'Let's ride, Frank,' he called. 'Reckon it's time we were goin'.' He turned to look down at the others stretched out beside the fire. 'The rest o' you stay awake and keep your eyes and ears open. Mebbe there ain't many ridin' these trails at night but don't take any chances.'

'When d'yuh figger you'll be back, Brett?' Seth enquired.

'Long afore dawn,' came the reply. 'And don't get trigger-happy when we ride up.'

Brett saddled his mount and checked the chambers of his Colts before pushing the guns back in their holsters. He didn't reckon on meeting with any trouble. Just a quick, careful check on the town, get the general lay-out registered in his mind, and find a couple of places where he might settle Frank and Ed when the time came.

Utter silence closed in around them as they headed down the steep slope. The tall trees hid everything from view in all directions. Not until they reached the bottom, where the narrow track met the trail leading into Bitter River, were they able to see any sign of the sky.

In front of them, less than a mile away, lay the darker shadow of the town. Brett reined up his mount and sat tall in the saddle, allowing his keen gaze to take in everything. Even at that early hour of the morning, a couple of pale yellow gleams were visible. He made a mental note of them.

The single street passed straight through the town with boardwalks on either side. Hitching rails edged the boardwalks but there were no horses tethered to them.

Brett pointed along the trail.

'We take the horses and then leave them outside town. The rest o' the way we go on foot.'

Franks's face was a pale blur in the dimness.

'And if we have to get outa there mighty quick?'

'We won't, if you do exactly as I say. Now let's get movin'.'

They gigged their mounts slowly forward, halting them while they were some distance from the nearest building. They stepped down and led the horses a short distance from the trail.

Hugging the walls of the low building as closely as possible so as not to expose themselves to anyone watching from the opposite side of the street, they crossed a gap between two squat buildings in half a dozen strides.

Brett breathed a little more easily now as he crouched down beside his brother in the shadows, flicking his gaze from side to side, every nerve and sense pushed to the limit, ready for the slightest hint of danger from any quarter.

The next buildings all sat very close together. One was evidently the jailhouse from the sign he could see just above the door. Some distance further on was one of the saloons. A pale gleam came from its windows and threw shadows across the boardwalk outside.

'I'll check this side o' the street,' he hissed softly to his companion. 'Wait until I give the word, then you make it to the other side.'

Frank nodded and waited. Then at a signal from Brett he darted across the street, doubled over, and melted into the shadows on the far boardwalk. Brett saw him glide swiftly towards a narrow alley that ran alongside a two-storey building which he guessed was the solitary hotel.

Once he had gone, Brett eased himself to his feet. There was still plenty of time to stake out the town. He had already decided which way they would enter for the final showdown. What he had to do now was locate the best positions in which to place Ed and Frank, from which they could have the drop on the sheriff from the rear. Somewhere on a roof or a top storey where they would have the best view of everything going on in the street.

He turned and padded silently along the narrow alley which led to the rear of the jail. Something moved swiftly in the shadows and his Colt was in his hand, finger tight on the trigger, before he saw it was nothing more than a mangy dog.

Cursing softly under his breath he realized that, for some reason, he was getting edgy.

He stepped back a little way and ran his questing gaze along the backs of the buildings. Only the one he had picked out as the bank had two storeys and that was out of the question. In broad daylight there would be too many people in its vicinity for one of the brothers to slip in unnoticed and make his way towards the upper rooms.

Then, dimly, he made out the squat outlines of a large building at the far end of the street. The livery stables, he guessed. Still treading cautiously, he picked his way through the darkness.

Five minutes later, he was at the front corner of the stables, his shoulder pressed tightly against the wall. He paused for a moment, then risked a quick look along the street. It stretched away in front of him, empty and with no sign of movement anywhere.

On reaching the stable doors, he slowly twisted the handle. They were unlocked and within seconds he had moved inside. Here there was utter blackness which contained nothing but the soft, nervous movements of the horses stabled there.

Feeling his way along the front of the stalls, he reached the far end. He paused to allow his eyes to adjust to the blackness and just made out the long ladder which led to the upper half of the building. The space at the top was filled with straw bales: feed for the animals.

A pale square of sky told him where the window was. Going over to it, he peered out. With a sense of satisfaction, he realized that this position afforded an unrestricted view of the entire street.

From there, it would be possible for a man to get a clear shot at anyone forty feet below.

On the other side of the street, Frank Kelton had reached the rear of the hotel. No lights showed in any of the windows and he reckoned everyone inside was asleep.

He found a large open space at the back with piles of rubbish from the hotel heaped against a low wall. Cautiously, keeping an eye on the hotel windows for any movement, he moved away until he had a full view along the entire length of the buildings. Most of the houses, he guessed, were occupied. But at the far end he spotted one, larger than the others, which appeared to be abandoned. Nodding to himself, he went back and moved along the side of the wall, cursing softly as his foot snagged against a heap of empty cans.

A faint, furtive sound outside his window woke Denvers from a light sleep. It had sounded like a foot striking metal. Within seconds, he was on his feet and at the window, his mind going back to the time when he had spotted a dark figure there; an incident which had led to the killing of those three gunslingers from the Double K.

At first, he could see nothing. Then a quick movement at the edge of his vision caught his attention. As deputy, it was his duty to check out anything suspicious in town. Within a minute, he had pulled on his shirt and trousers and was buckling on his gunbelt.

He slipped on his boots and made his way quietly out of his room and down the creaking stairs. For a moment, he debated whether to wake Manders, then decided to let him sleep. The sheriff had plenty on his mind.

A blast of cold night air hit him as he stepped outside and worked his way around to the rear. There was now no sign of the prowler but it was not in him to hesitate. He doubted if it had been any of Dawson's hired hands and if the Kelton brothers were anywhere in the vicinity, they'd come riding in together, not go skulking around in the shadows.

At each narrow alley-mouth, he paused and examined the dark shadows. Then, not far away, someone stirred. The sound was only just audible, the clink of metal against a wall as if someone wearing spurs had moved slowly away from him.

He pulled himself up into taut immobility and listened intently, trying to gauge exactly where the other man was. It seemed unlikely that the prowler was aware of his presence.

The seconds passed with an agonizing slowness. He slid his gun into his right hand and stepped into the alley-mouth. As he had expected, the man stood with his back to him some ten feet away. He was just an anonymous shape in the darkness.

Lining up the gun barrel on the man's back, he spoke softly.

'Just hold it right there, friend. And keep your hand away from your gun.'

He saw the other stiffen abruptly, evidently taken completely by surprise. For a moment, he thought the man intended to make his play in spite of his having the drop on him. Then he relaxed his shoulders fractionally and lifted his hand away from his gun.

'Right. Now step back and keep your hands where I can see 'em.'

Moving back a couple of paces, Denvers watched warily as the man edged back along the alley.

'You got nothin' on me, whoever you are,' grated the other harshly. 'Just who are you?'

'You'll find that out soon enough. Either you're here to kill someone, or you've already done it. Whichever it is, I guess I'd better lock you up for the night. You can answer some questions in the mornin'.'

Denvers saw the man's body tighten at that remark. The other was only a couple of feet in front of him when the man suddenly flung himself to one side. In the same instant, his right foot kicked savagely back against Denvers' knee. Pain jarred redly through his leg as spurs raked across his flesh.

Dimly, Denvers was aware that the other was running swiftly towards the far end of the alley. Stumbling awkwardly, he steadied himself against the wall with his left hand, bringing up the Colt. Both of his shots ricocheted off the wall in the distance and a moment later, the man had vanished around the corner.

Sucking air into his lungs, Uenvers moved as quickly as he could along the alley. He thought he detected a vague shadow in the distance but whoever it was, Denvers guessed he had a horse waiting near the edge of town.

With an effort, he made his way back to the hotel to find Steve standing just inside the doorway. The proprietor stood beside him.

'I heard a couple of shots,' Steve said. He glanced down at the other's leg. 'What the hell happened?'

'I heard someone moving around outside and went for a look-see. I figgered that, whoever he was, he was up to no good. Caught him in one o' the alleys yonder.'

'You get a look at him?'

Denvers shook his head. 'Nope. He had his back to me all the time. I had the drop on him but he raked his spurs across my leg and got away. He could be anywhere by now.'

'Can't be helped. You see anyone else around?'

'No one. I figger he was a loner. But he was prowlin' around for a reason.'

Steve thought that over. His first intuitive thought was that the Kelton brothers might have ridden into town under cover of darkness to set up an ambush for him.

'If you want my opinion,' put in the proprietor, 'I'd say it was the Nangordo Kid. Talk is he's headed this way to join with the Keltons.'

Steve considered that for a moment. It made sense although from what he'd heard about this outlaw, shooting a man down from ambush in an alley was not his style. His way was to call out his opponent on the street.

'Better get the doc to take a look at that.' Steve turned to the short, balding man beside him. 'Run over and bring Doc Marsden back here.'

'Hell, it ain't nothin' but a flesh wound,' Denvers protested.

Steve ignored him. 'Get Marsden here right away. He's sure to be awake. I guess most o' the town heard that gunfire.'

The proprietor was back within ten minutes with the doctor at his back.

Marsden led Denvers inside and waited while the proprietor brought a couple of lanterns and placed them on the table in the dining-room. The wound was not large but it had bled a lot.

'Get me a basin of hot water,' Marsden ordered. 'I'll clean it up for you. Don't reckon it'll hinder you too much.'

'Good.'

'Who was it, one o' those outlaws that Dawson's hired?'

Steve glanced up. Mary stood in the doorway. Evidently she, too, had been wakened by the shots. There was an expression of deep concern on her face.

'We don't know who it was,' Steve told her. 'Denvers

didn't get a look at his face.'

Mary gave him a direct look. 'Can you think of any reason why anyone should be skulking around town at this time of the morning, unless they were here to kill someone?'

'Nope.' Sheve shook his head. 'But why would one o' the Kelton brothers come here like that? When they ride in, they'll come in a bunch. That's the way these gunslingers operate.' Steve's face was like flint as he added: 'Could've been the Nangordo Kid takin' stock o' the town.'

Mary's eyes flicked towards the deputy. 'Do you reckon that might be the case?'

Denvers gave a wry smile. 'I've seen plenty o' Wanted posters out for him south of here and along the border. But it was too dark in that alley for me even to hazard a guess.'

Marsden finished bandaging his leg.

'A couple of days and that should be fully healed,' he said. 'Lucky for you the rowel didn't go through to the bone or you'd have been laid up for a week.'

On the edge of town Frank Kelton waited impatiently for his brother to return. The horses were getting restive and he knew those two shots would have alerted all of the townsfolk. Even at that moment, the sheriff might be getting a posse rounded up and those were odds he didn't fancy.

He had no doubts about the identity of the man who'd got the drop on him in that alley. Even though he hadn't seen him, the fact that he'd intended jailing him told him all he wanted to know.

He rolled a cigarette and he leaned against a nearby tree, keeping a sharp eye on the town. From where he stood, he could clearly see everything going on but there was no sign of any riders mounting up. Either they had decided it wasn't worth the trouble riding out after him or that sheriff was unable to get anyone willing to ride with him.

Eventually he decided there was going to be no pursuit. He relaxed a little. But his hand was shaking slightly as he applied the match to his smoke. He fought to control himself before Brett came back.

Where the hell was he? It occurred to him that his brother might be holed up somewhere, unable to move until all of the excitement had died down. Then there came a faint sound from somewhere to his left and a moment later Brett emerged from the shadows at the edge of the trail.

'Were you the cause of all that ruckus?' Brett demanded angrily. 'You could've brought the whole town down on our necks.'

Before Frank could reply Brett went on harshly, speaking through his teeth. 'I said we was to go in there, pick out a couple o' likely places for two of you to hide, and we'd get out without anyone knowin' we'd been there.'

'Weren't no fault o' mine, Brett. That damned sheriff came on me from behind. How was I to know he patrols the town?'

' 'Course it was your fault.' Without warning, Brett's fist swung out, catching Frank on the side of the jaw. He fell back against the tree. 'Damn you. Why didn't you make sure there was no one around? You could've got us both killed. As it is, we're lucky they didn't decide to come after us. And how do you know it was the sheriff?'

'Couldn't have been anyone else. He was threatening to lock me in jail when I made my play.'

'All right, damn you. Now get on your mount and let's get back to the others.'

Back in his room, Steve sat on the edge of the bed and tried to think things out. What had happened tonight had disturbed him. He'd expected Dawson to lie low and keep quiet until he was ready to send in those killers. So just who was the man Denvers had caught prowling around in the darkness, evidently not wanting to be seen?

The Nangordo Kid? It was possible but, somehow, it didn't fit in with what little he knew about this gun-crazed hellion. Only a few hours earlier, he had gone through the Wanted posters in his desk. He'd come across three with pictures of Brett, Matt and Seth Kelton.

Now he took them out of his pocket and placed them on the small bedside table, drawing the lamp a little closer.

He had found nothing relating to the two remaining brothers but he reckoned that if Dawson had got word to one of them, the other two would be with them, expecting a share of the money Dawson was willing to pay them.

A soft knock on the door brought him swiftly to his feet. He picked up the Colt from the bed and walked quietly to the door, then jerked it open, bringing up the barrel of the gun. He lowered it quickly as he saw

Denvers standing there.

'Figgered you might still be awake,' Denvers said.

Steve motioned him inside, threw a glance along the corridor, then closed the door.

'You got somethin' on your mind?' he asked, gesturing towards the chair.

'Somethin' that just came to me about that *hombre* I jumped tonight.'

'What was that?'

'I got the feelin' he was lookin' for something. He seemed to be checking on the building on this side o' the street. When I eventually tracked him down, he was movin' along the side o' that empty place right at the far end o' the street.'

'As if he was lookin' for some place to hole up?'

'Could be. I figger if he was in town to kill someone, he'd have had a drawn gun in his hand.'

'Take a look at these.' Steve handed the Wanted posters to his deputy. 'I know it ain't likely since you never saw his face but . . .'

Denvers studied the three faces, then shook his head.

'I'm fairly sure it weren't any o' these. I'd say this gunslinger was a younger man.'

'It was just a chance.' Steve rubbed his chin thoughtfully. 'I reckon that leads me to only one conclusion. There's only one other gunhawk likely to be roamin' the town lookin' for a place where he can shoot me in the back.'

'The Nangordo Kid.'

'You know anythin' about him? There's nothin' in any of the information I've got on men wanted by the law in this neck o' the woods.'

'Far as I know, he's wanted in about every town and state south of here and all along the Mexico border. Mostly rides alone. Stage hold-ups and bank robbery. Most o' those he's killed have been young gunslicks who've gone up against him in a straight fight, reckonin' on getting a reputation as the one who outdrew him.'

Denvers got to his feet and went to the door. 'Reckon we both need some sleep.' he said. 'Somehow, I doubt if that night prowler will be back.'

The next morning Steve noticed the small knot of men and women standing just outside his office. His first thought was that they had come to enquire about the happenings of the night. They moved aside and let him step up on to the boardwalk. There was no doubting the hostility on several of their faces.

Inside the office, he found Denvers waiting for him. The deputy jerked a thumb towards the crowd.

'Looks to me like some o' the citizens are pretty het up about somethin', Sheriff.'

Through the open door, Steve eyed the people outside. Most of them he recognized. He noticed Clive Donalds, the bank manager, in the forefront, his gold watch and chain glinting in the sunlight. Behind him were others, members of the town committee.

Steve stepped outside.

'What's all this about?' he asked. 'If it's about what happened last night, there was—'

'It ain't just last night, Sheriff,' the banker said huskily. 'This is about what's goin' to happen in this town when those outlaws ride in. All right, Manders, you're a damned good sheriff and I agree you did get almost all of that stolen money back – and for that, I'm grateful.'

'I also got the gang who held you up at gunpoint,' Steve reminded him.

'We had a meetin' last night,' called another of the men. 'We hadn't got nothin' personal against you. But we've got to live here with our wives and children. Once those killers come, ain't no way o' tellin' what they'll do.

'Slim Benson saw sense when he handed in his badge. Now you've only got this stranger to stand with you and we don't know a damned thing about him. If he has any savvy, he'll quit too.'

'If any one of you had any guts, you'd back the sheriff.' Denvers spoke up from the doorway at Steve's back. 'This is your town but unless you stand up and fight for it, it's goin' to become a helltown.'

'I suggest you keep outa this,' snapped the other, edging forward until he stood close to the hitching rail. 'These killers have nothin' against the townsfolk o' Bitter River. This is personal between them and the sheriff. We reckon that if he leaves town right now, they'll ride on and—'

'And leave this place in peace?' Sarcasm edged Steve's tone. 'If you think that, then you're all fools. They'll take this place apart, together with all the money and gold you've got in the bank.'

'That's jest what we expected you to say, Sheriff.' Chet Hogan, the saloon-owner spoke up from the side of the crowd. 'This feud you had with Cal Dawson started all o' this. Now there ain't no stoppin' Clem and those killers he's hired. You figger that you and this gunslick deputy can take on the Keltons and the Nangordo Kid? They'll shoot you down like dogs.'

'And then they'll turn on us,' called one of the women. 'We elected you as sheriff to keep law and order in town, not bring in outlaws.'

'Then why don't you stand by him?' Doc Marsden's voice rang out over the crowd. 'These killers only thrive because decent people won't stand up to them and fight.'

'Fight!' Donalds turned on the doctor. 'How do you expect folk like us to fight these killers? We're not gunmen.'

'I'll stand with you, Sheriff.'

Steve glanced up. Seb Butler had approached and was standing with a shotgun in his hands, his grizzled face glaring contempt at the others. 'If these folk are too yeller to fight for their rights, I'll back you.'

Steve forced a wry grin. 'Thanks for the offer, old-timer. But I reckon you'd better stay outa this.'

'You reckon I'm so old I can't handle this?' Butler declared indignantly. 'Ain't nothin' wrong with my sight that I can't blast two or three o' them killers to hell.'

'I'm sure you can, Seb. But it'll be best if you leave this to us.'

Most of the men had fallen silent at Butler's outburst. Then Hogan spoke up once more.

'Don't listen to him. I know we elected him sheriff but that don't mean we can't take his badge away and put somebody else in his place, somebody these killers ain't interested in.'

'And another thing,' called one of the men at the back of the crowd. 'Who gave you the right to deputize this stranger? We know nothin' about him. Comes ridin' into town out o' nowhere. He's got the look of a killer himself.'

'I deputized him,' Steve said harshly. 'Seems he's the only one in town apart from Seb who has any stomach for a fight.' He recognized that these men were frightened and with good reason. And frightened men were liable to take extreme measures to protect themselves. But he knew full well that if they had their way and he left like a coward, Bitter River was finished.

Clem Dawson would take over everything. His word would be law and whoever became sheriff in his place would take orders only from the rancher.

CHAPTER NINE

GUNFIRE AT NOON

Staring out across the crowd, Steve could see that more and more of the citizens were lining up behind Donalds and Hogan, backing their demand that he should stand down as sheriff and leave town. He knew that within a few days at most the lines would be drawn and it would all be over – finished, one way or another.

He was aware he had only two choices. To stand up to these outlaws and force these people to recognize that they too had a duty if they wanted a town free from corruption and banditry – or he would have to accept their wishes and ride out. Whether Mary would come with him, still want to marry a man on the run, he wasn't sure.

Before he could say anything, the doctor spoke up.

'I believe the sheriff is right. Forcin' him out of office ain't going to solve anything. Once Clem Dawson gets his way this town won't be worth livin' in. I say we have to back Sheriff Manders.'

'We want to see law and order here,' Hogan yelled fiercely. 'But I'm not prepared to have the whole town shot up, mebbe several of us killed in the process.'

'Then I guess you'd better get used to it,' Steve snapped. 'As far as bein' sheriff, I don't have to look to my actions for any justification. No matter what you say, I'm stayin' on as the law here. Now I suggest you all leave and go about your normal business.'

He turned on his heel and went back into the office, aware that Denvers and the doctor had followed him.

'They seem pretty riled up about this,' Denvers commented. 'The whole town is on its toes.'

'I'll talk to them,' Marsden promised. 'They might listen to me. From what I saw there are just two or three ringleaders tryin' to stir things up. The rest will follow like sheep.'

'I'm stayin', Doc. No matter what anyone says,' Steve retorted.

'Then it's time they learned they've got to sacrifice somethin' if there's ever to be peace in Bitter River. This town ain't goin' to grow and prosper if Clem Dawson gets his hands on it.'

A glimpse through the window told Steve that most of the townsfolk had dispersed. Only Hogan and a couple of other men were in the street outside. They were talking animatedly among themselves. Over on the far side of the street, Seb Butler was standing near the alley, his shotgun cradled in his arms.

'Keep your eyes open, Steve,' the doctor said as he went out. 'Some of 'em are still in an ugly mood. They might take it into their heads to try somethin'.'

'I'll be ready for 'em if they do,' Steve said softly.

Denvers lowered himself into a nearby chair and placed his legs on the desk. In spite of the trouble that was looming, he seemed quite at ease.

Once again, Steve wondered about this man and his old score with Clem Dawson. If that was all he had on his mind, he mused, why hadn't he simply ridden out to the Double K and settled things with Dawson the moment he'd ridden into town and knew where the rancher was? Even if the law eventually caught up with him, he doubted if any jury would have convicted him once they knew the full story.

Before he could ask the question, Denvers asked one of his own.

'You must have known for some time these killers were ridin' in to get you, Sheriff. Why didn't you send for the federal marshal? There could've been a posse here by now to take care of 'em without you havin' to risk your neck.'

'Don't think I didn't consider it. But there was only one man I could trust at the time. My deputy, Slim Benson. And Dawson had every trail out o' town watched. If I'd sent him for the nearest marshal, he'd never have made it.' He levered himself to his feet. 'Guess I'll go for a drink. You care to come with me?'

Denvers shook his head. 'Reckon I'll stay here and keep an eye on the place, if you don't mind.'

Shrugging, Steve left and made his way along the boardwalk towards the saloon. He couldn't fail to notice the animosity on the faces of the few people he passed.

Even though it was mid-morning, there were a dozen men there, all gathered at the far end.

'You want a drink, Sheriff?' asked the bartender.

Steve nodded. 'Whiskey,' he said shortly. He took the bottle and glass which the other slid along the counter towards him. Then he called the man over.

'Hogan anywhere around?' he asked.

'Over yonder with the others.' The bartender's tone was low as if not wanting to be overheard.

Steve turned his head and saw the saloon owner's bulky figure seated against the far wall. Hogan said something and a few of the heads turned in Steve's direction.

'Reckon you got most o' the town against you, Sheriff,' muttered the bartender.

'So I understand. But I figger that's all talk.'

'You think those outlaws are really on their way to get you, or is this just bluff on Dawson's part?' The bartender did not meet Steve's eyes, as if he already knew what the answer would be.

'They're comin',' Steve said as he poured some of the whiskey into the glass. 'Today, tomorrow, or the day after. But they'll be here.'

'Hellfire. And you stickin' around just waitin' for it to happen?' The bartender eyed him in astonished surprise. 'Goddamnit, Sheriff! If I was in your shoes I'd be over the border by now.'

Steve downed the drink and poured himself another.

'There are worse ways for a man to die.' he said.

It was just on sundown when the five men left their hideout in the hills and rode down the twisting, tortuous trail out of the trees. By now, Brett was getting impatient. The sight of all that money which the rancher had shown them had made him eager to get his hands on it, finish this job, and get away.

In spite of Dawson's insistence that all trails out of Bitter River were still being watched and not even a rat could slip through to pass on warning of their presence to the law outside, he was still nervous.

For most of the way, they rode in an uneasy silence, eyes and ears alert. Not until they reached the river did Frank speak.

'You still certain this fella Dawson is on the level, Brett?'

Without turning his head, Brett muttered: 'He's got to be. One thing is for sure. There ain't any other lawmen in that town. And without our help in gettin' rid o' this sheriff, he'll never avenge his son or get control o' that town.'

Lights showed in several of the windows as they rode up. For a moment, a shadow appeared against one of the lower windows and a minute later the door opened and Dawson stood framed against the light from the lantern he held in his right hand.

'Step this way,' he called. 'You sure you weren't followed?'

Brett grinned savagely. 'Do you take us for fools?'

'No, I guess not.' Dawson gestured them inside, closed the door, and led them into the large room. He placed the lamp on the desk and motioned them to be seated.

Looking from one to the other, he spoke tersely.

'I've reached my decision. Noon tomorrow.'

Brett nodded, satisfied. That suited him perfectly. He had no wish to remain any longer in this territory.

'And the rest o' the money? When do we get that?'

'Like I said before. Just as soon as the job's finished.'

Before Brett could speak, Matt spoke up.

'The way I see it, Dawson, it would be better if we were to have it now.'

'When the job is done and Manders is lyin' dead in the middle o' the street. That was our agreement.'

Matt's hand moved to his side. His thin lips were drawn back across his teeth.

'Mebbe you're still tryin' to double-cross us, Dawson.'

'Why should I do that? I'll ride in some ways behind you, then you make your way back here. I ain't goin' to run and leave this place, am I? I've too much at stake here.'

Matt drew his Colt and laid it on the table in front of him. There was a bright glint in his eyes which Dawson noticed at once. He swallowed thickly.

'You won't kill me,' he said. 'Only dynamite will open that safe without the combination. Kill me and you'll never know it.'

'Jest simmer down, Matt.' Brett spoke without taking his glance from Dawson's face. 'And put that gun away.'

Something ominous had come over Matt's face. Now it entered his voice. The expression in his eyes boded ill for the rancher.

'I know ways o' makin' you talk, Dawson,' he grated. He turned to his elder brother. 'Why risk our hides against this sheriff when we can just take the money and ride out? We ain't got no guarantee that money is still in the safe. He could be stringin' us along.'

'Matt's right,' Ed said. 'And for all we know there

147

could be plenty o' men in that town ready to fight.'

Brett's big fist hammered loudly on the table.

'I'm the one who says what we do and what we don't.' His voice was as rigid as an iron bar. 'Any o' you don't like it can ride out now. But you'll take none o' the money with you.'

Across the table, Dawson relaxed slightly in his chair. For some reason, he felt he could trust the big man facing him to go through with the deal. But he knew he was in a precarious position as regards the others.

For a moment, the ugly glint in Matt's eyed boded further argument. Then he shrugged slightly, picked up the Colt and thrust it angrily into its holster. Through his clenched teeth, he muttered:

'All right, Brett. But if anythin' goes wrong . . .' He deliberately left the remainder of his sentence unsaid but there was a note of ill-concealed menace behind his words.

Sitting back, Dawson asked: 'You prepared to ride in tomorrow at noon?'

Drawing back his lips, Brett showed his large teeth in a broad smile.

'That suits us fine. We've already staked out the town. Ain't no chance in hell o' this lawman livin' after noon.'

'Good. Once that's finished, you'll be paid as we agreed. One thing's for sure. With Manders dead, there'll be nobody on your trail.'

After the others had gone, Dawson lit a cigar and went outside on to the veranda. He'd played a big gamble bringing these outlaws in but it had certainly paid off in the end. Things had gone exactly as he had hoped. By this time tomorrow, he'd have no problems with the townsfolk.

Once he got them to elect a new sheriff and deputies of his choosing, any of the smaller spreads would fall into his hands. Either he'd force them to sell out at a fraction of their worth, or he'd run them out of the territory.

His only regret was that he now had no son to leave his empire to and carry on his name. And that was another thing Manders would pay for with his life.

The sun had been up for little over an hour the next morning when Matt and Frank Kelton left the cave deep in the hills and rode out for Bitter River. They rode quickly but cautiously, not expecting to meet anyone on the trail until they came within sight of the town.

The plan had been worked out in detail by Brett during the night and each man knew exactly what he had to do. Half an hour later, they reined up a little way from town and left their mounts among the trees. They anticipated no pursuit once they rode out.

As they eased the Colts in their holsters Matt pointed off to their right. Their plan now was to approach the town from either side, reaching the livery stables and abandoned storehouse from the rear. With luck, they reckoned they could reach their chosen hiding places without being seen by anyone in town.

Bitter River lay in a shallow valley surrounded by open brushland which would afford them with plenty of cover.

Frank made to move off, then halted as Matt spoke harshly.

'Remember Brett's orders. No shootin' until he gives the signal.'

'I've got it,' Frank snapped. Without another word, he cut across the trail and vanished into the trees on the other side.

Once he'd gone, Matt set off through the pines and out on to the open scrubland which bordered the town. There was plenty of activity in the street. Occasionally he saw figures passing along at the far ends of the narrow alleys that radiated outward from it.

He knew he was gambling on no one glancing along one of those alleys but that was a risk he had to take. Doubled over, he ran from one clump of scrub to another. Eventually he gained the rear of the livery stables, gasping air into his heaving chest.

Working his way around the side, he glanced warily along the street. At that time of the morning, there were plenty of folk on the boardwalks but fortunately this end of town was almost deserted.

Within seconds, he was inside the stables, narrowing his eyes against the dark shadows. At first, he thought the place was deserted apart from the handful of horses. Then, without warning, a figure stepped out of one of the stalls.

The man saw him instantly.

'You come for your mount, mister?' He stepped towards Matt.

Matt nodded. Stepping up to the man he motioned with one hand towards the far stall. Unsuspecting, the other half-turned his head. Before he could look back, Matt's gun was in his hand, the barrel between his clenched fingers. The butt struck the man heavily on

150

the side of the head.

Matt caught him as he fell and dragged him out of sight into the nearest empty stall. Whether the man was dead or merely unconscious made no difference to him. Swiftly, he climbed the ladder to the top floor and settled himself to wait at the window.

At almost the same time Frank Kelton was working his way up to the flat roof of the derelict building opposite the stables. From there he wormed his way forward to a position where he could draw a bead on anyone down in the street. Looking across, he caught the glint of sunlight where it struck off the weapon in his brother's hand at the window.

Down below, everything went on as normal. Matt watched the scene idly, his lips curling into a faintly sneering smile. Very soon, he thought, all of that would change.

Staying in the middle of the dusty street, Steve let his keen glance roam over the buildings on either side. The tension inside him had been building up since dawn. Many of the folk on the boardwalks stared at him in sullen silence as he walked slowly towards the end of town.

He had no way of knowing when these hired killers would ride in for the final showdown. Evidently, Dawson was being true to his word and making him sweat.

Out of the corner of his eye he saw the doctor come out of his surgery. Noticing him, Marsden walked over.

'You seem to be expectin' trouble today, Steve. You're a mite more jumpy than usual.'

'Those polecats ain't goin' to wait long. The longer they stick around here, the more chance of 'em running into a federal marshal or a gang o' bounty hunters on the hunt for 'em. And I don't reckon they'll wait until dark. They like to call a man out in daylight where everyone can see.'

'You reckon that stranger will stick with you when the time comes? After all, it ain't his fight.'

'Somehow, I think he will. There's somethin' burning deep inside that man, somethin' I can't figger out.'

Marsden ran a hand down his face. 'If he does, it'll even things up. From my judgement of him, he could be mighty handy with a gun.'

Steve opened his mouth to say something more but at that moment, there came a sudden shout from the end of the street. Seb Butler came into view.

'They're comin'.' His voice was a throaty yell. 'I jest seen 'em along the trail. About half a mile away.'

'How many?' Steve called.

'Only three of 'em.'

'You sure?'

The old-timer nodded emphatically. 'Danged sure, Sheriff.'

'Then that could mean Dawson only managed to get three o' the Keltons, or—'

'Or there are already two of the critters already holed up somewhere in town,' Marsden finished.

A door closed loudly further along the street and Denvers came over, fastening his gunbelt. He had his Winchester over his shoulders.

Most of the townsfolk had already heard Butler's warning shout and were moving hastily inside the nearby buildings, well away from the doors and windows.

'I'll get my scattergun,' Butler said.

'You'll get outa sight along with the others,' Steve told him firmly. 'I don't want to have to watch out for you when these sidewinders ride in.'

For a moment, he thought the old-timer was going to argue. Then Butler turned reluctantly and walked off.

Suddenly, the town was very quiet.

With Denvers standing a little way behind him, Steve waited. At the far end of town, the trail was still empty.

The minutes passed with a dragging slowness, heightening the tension in the still air.

Then there was a movement in the distance and the three riders came into sight. They rode in slowly, sitting tall in the saddle. They pulled up their mounts alongside the far tethering rail. As if Steve and Denvers didn't exist, they looped the reins over the rail, then moved away into the middle of the street, strung out across it with the biggest of the three in the centre.

They halted while still thirty feet away, their hands held loosely at their sides.

'I see you're a bigger fool than I took you for, Sheriff,' shouted Brett. 'I had you figgered for a yeller coward who'd run once he knew we were ridin' into town. Guess I was wrong.'

'Reckon you don't know how wrong you are,' Steve called back. He knew the other was trying to goad him into going for his guns.

Seth uttered a braying laugh. 'See you've managed to get some other fool to stand by you. Won't make a spit o' difference. This is where you both die.'

Brett started walking slowly forward and a second later, the other two followed. Tensing himself, Steve unfocused his eyes, his gaze taking in all three men.

'Just keep your eye on those three, Sheriff,' Denvers said in a low whisper. 'I'll watch your back.'

His back to Steve's, he stood facing the opposite end of the street. He could see nothing but instinct told him there were two killers there, waiting for a signal to gun them down. Clearly, they had expected only one man facing them.

He heard the shout from behind him.

'All right, Manders. Let's see how fast you are with those guns o' yours.'

In the same instant, Denvers saw the two figures, high up on opposite sides of the street. Like lightning, the Winchester was in his hands. It roared twice, the sound of the shots echoing along the street. Matt Kelton suddenly jerked and slumped forward over the low sill of the window, his gun falling from nerveless fingers.

In almost the same instant, Frank teetered back on his heels as the bullet took him in the chest. Somehow, he got off a single shot that smashed through the window of the bank before he toppled from the high roof. His body turned over twice before he hit the boardwalk below.

Denvers dropped his rifle in the dust and whirled swiftly, his Colts clearing leather in a blur of motion. Brett Kelton was swaying on his feet, his mouth slack, a look of stupefied amazement on his coarse features as Steve's slug hit him squarely in the chest.

Seth and Ed had their guns clear of the holsters

when the twin Colts in Denvers' hands spat gunflame. Ed went back on his heels and crashed into the dust on his back, eyes staring blindly at the sky. Seth remained poised on his feet, swaying drunkenly.

With the last ounce of life left in him, he struggled to raise his gun. Steve went forward, levelling his Colt, but there was no need for a further shot. Pitching forward on to his face, his legs twisted awkwardly, Seth lay sprawled against the edge of the boardwalk.

Doc Marsden came running out with Mary on his heels. He stared hard at Denvers.

'Hellfire and damnation,' he said tightly. 'That sure was some mighty slick shootin'. I ain't never seen anythin' like it.' He stared along the street in bewilderment at the bodies of Matt and Frank Kelton.

'All that remains now is to bring Dawson in for trial,' Steve said shortly. 'I don't reckon we'll have much trouble linkin' him with this bunch.'

'Dawson's mine,' Denvers said sharply.

'You got somethin' on him?' Marsden asked. 'Somehow I figured you didn't just ride into this town to help the sheriff against these hellions.'

'I have a chore to finish.' Without another word, Denvers spun on his heel and headed for the livery stables.

He came back five minutes later, leading his mount by the bridle.

'You're going to kill him,' Mary said.

Denvers' smile was not a nice thing.

'That's right, ma'am,' he replied. 'Just like he killed my brother durin' the war. Took him into the rocks and shot him down in cold blood.'

'Reckon you should leave that to a judge and jury,' Steve said.

Denvers shook his head. 'That ain't good enough, Sheriff. I have to do this my way and—'

'Looks like you might get your chance right now,' the doctor said, turning his head.

There was the sound of riders coming in from the direction of the Double K ranch. A few seconds later Clem Dawson rode in with a bunch of his men at his back.

He reined up so sharply that his horse almost threw him as he saw Steve standing there and the strewn bodies lying in the dust.

'You're finished, Dawson,' Steve called loudly. 'Guess you played your trump card and lost.'

Beneath the tan, Dawson's face had turned ashen. His wide-eyed gaze passed over the dead men lying in front of him as he struggled to accept that his carefully laid plan had failed.

Then he jerked himself upright.

'Damn you, Manders. I don't know how you did this but I ain't finished yet.' His hand went for the gun at his waist. He drew it swiftly and levelled it at Steve.

'Oh yes, you are.' Denvers stepped into view from the side of his mount.

At the sight of him, Dawson's eyes widened in sudden shock.

'You!' Somehow, he got the word out. 'How the devil did you. . . ?'

He suddenly ducked his head, threw himself sideways in the saddle. He swung the gun, aiming it at Denvers.

In his haste, his shot went wide, ricocheting with a thin screech off the wall of the jail. Within a split second, Denvers fired a single shot from the hip. The slug took the rancher between the eyes.

Spooked by the sound, his mount bolted, dragging its rider with it. Dawson's body hung limply on one side as the horse dragged him through the dust, his boot caught in the stirrup.

Steve faced the bunch of riders. 'You men ride outa town unless you want locked up in jail,' he said harshly. 'Don't any of you come back to Bitter River.' He knew there was no fight left in them. Wheeling their mounts, they headed towards the trail.

Denvers holstered his gun and climbed into the saddle. He took the badge from his shirt, bent down and handed it to Steve.

'Reckon my job here is finished, Sheriff. I'll be ridin' on.'

'You're welcome to stay here,' the doctor put in. 'After what I've just seen, you'd make a damned good deputy. Besides, there's still the—' He broke off sharply as Mary put a hand on his arm.

Stepping forward, she stared up at Denvers. There was a strange look in her eyes.

'I prayed for a miracle once,' she said. 'Just who are you? Somehow, I've got a feeling that Denvers isn't your real name.'

The man in the saddle gave a brief smile.

'Guess I figgered the whole town knew after what Dawson told the sheriff. My friends call me Frank Denvers. South o' here and along the border, they know me as the Nangordo Kid.'

Touching the brim of his hat with his hand, he said quietly: '*Adios* ma'am. *Adios* Sheriff. Somehow, I don't think our trails will cross again.'

Putting spurs to his mount, he rode slowly along the narrow street without a backward glance.

'You heard him, Sheriff,' Marsden said hoarsely. 'Ain't you goin' to arrest him. He's a wanted outlaw.'

Steve was silent for a moment, then shook his head.

'Nope. Not because for once in his life he put himself on the side o' the law, but because the only way to take him in would be to shoot him in the back. And I ain't ever done that. Let him go. There's been enough bloodshed here for one day.'

Placing his arm around Mary's waist, he walked slowly towards his office. Behind them, folk were coming out on to the street once more, the street of a town from which some evil cloud seemed to have just been lifted.